Dead is Dead,
but Not Always

by Eddie Generous

A HellBound Books Publishing LLC Book
Houston TX

A HellBound Books LLC
Publication

Copyright © 2018 by HellBound Books Publishing LLC

All Rights Reserved

Cover and art design by
Eddie Generous

Edited By Xtina Marie

www.hellboundbookspublishing.com

Printed in the United States of America

CONTENTS

The Howl
Of the Knoll
We, in the Dark, Together, Forever
Slithering
The Weight of Solitude, the Pressure of Conscience
Dead Lake
Over the Fields and Through the Woods

Dead is Dead, But Not Always

"*Dead is Dead, But Not Always* is a unique collection that thrills and illuminates. The prose is sharp and almost lyrical, the stories not your average fare. These are thoughtful, complex tales that transcend the concept of genre."

—Mark Allan Gunnells, author of *Companions in Ruin* and *The Cult of Ocasta*

"With cutting tales simultaneously ominous, brooding, and viscerally horrifying, Eddie Generous brings a welcome flair of originality to his newest collection. *Dead is Dead, but Not Always* digs into the surreal darkness of your worst nightmares and drags your demons shredding and clawing their way to the treacherous surface of reality."

—Shane Keene, HorrorTalk

Dead is Dead, But Not Always

Dead is Dead, but Not Always

Dead is Dead, But Not Always

The Howl

Some of the students whispered about monsters in the mountains, while others whispered about demons from underground.

The pale walls creaked and the winter winds keened through the gaps as if the knotty swirls whistled a tune. *Ghosts of the classroom*, the older students told the younger students, the same students talking about the monsters and demons. The only thing these tales of unseen forces had in common was bloodlust.

Ravijk, a valley town plopped into the center of the Keilkirk mountain range, had seventy-four residents, nineteen of these children. Sixteen of those children sat in their coats, the two space heaters doing little until the weather permitted the delivery of parts into the valley so that Ferdinand might repair the ancient furnace.

The spiders had gotten in and built a nest, Igne didn't understand why the janitor didn't just pull them out. Ferdinand explained nesting, homing, growing over decades, and becoming poisonous owners of spider farms. This meant that he had to burn the insulating lining and replace the bricks.

She still didn't get it.

"You don't want to see those little buggers all growed-up. Folks say they work with the beasts of the Howl," he said, grinning, expression sinister.

Therefore, the furnace remained busted until the parts arrived.

At the back of the room, the Guild triplets sat bare armed and hot amid their shivering classmates. Most avoided the triplets. Those girls were strange.

Nature in the valley town was like clockwork. Every three weeks or so the locals battened down against the gales. *Howlers* was the local name. Winter, spring, summer, and autumn, the Howlers came when they wanted and stayed a night. It had been almost four weeks since a Howler last pushed through the valley. Overdue.

"Girls, did you finish your reports?" Ms. Inge Dorthea asked and forced a smile.

It was her first teaching position, she'd grown up in the connected world, not used to the seclusion, but she liked the idea of mountain living, fresh air, visits from caribou, reindeer, and mountain goats.

The Guild girls fanned their cheeks, glowing red, blood aflame in their veins. They nodded and all pushed single sheets of lined paper forward.

Inge let the students choose their source books, anything they wanted, so long as she had a chance to read the book beforehand. This kept the kids interested. Interested kids are productive and she knew if she applied the right technique, she'd have a classroom of students excelling beyond the valley town.

She looked at the tight, neat lettering, Shelley's *Frankenstein* in three similar, yet different ways. "Are you girls all right?" she asked. The burning girls were alarming and curious.

"Fine," Eila, Eisa, and Ericka said in unison.

They were perfect students and that made them all the stranger. Despite her efforts, Inge did not yet have a class of excelling students.

Inge addressed six of the students, six to ten in age, and was just about to ask what four multiplied by three equalled when the wind howled, muting the question. The girls fanned wildly as the wind blew through the cracks, hot.

A daytime Howler.

The typically nocturnal display of power threw the teacher from her game plan and she stood dumbfounded, uncertain of how to progress. It was several ticks to three and the classroom listened in silence for twenty-minutes, feigning work efforts. Most students removed their coats. The heat had jumped up the thermometer with the hot wind. Sweat dripped down the pretty red-tinted faces of the triplets.

Inge yelled against the caterwaul, but to no avail. She pointed at the clock and mouthed *go home*. They understood and packed up their bags. The howler's warmth came down from the peaks of the Keilkirk range, from the east, pushing volcanic steam into the snowy valley.

After the students stepped out, Inge locked the classroom and walked home—a small cottage to the southern end of the village. The town hall hosted free movies nightly and Igne's plan, prior to the wind, was to partake. The film itself mattered none. Films were a gateway to other worlds, especially while living in seclusion. Of course, the raucous din put an axe to the option.

She listened to a selection of Mozart through her headphones that barely overstepped the howl. The snow melted as if spring had sprung. The heavy old trees danced and swayed with the wind. The space between the Earth and the stars was hazy.

Igne slept while Mozart's tunes roared, too warm, no sheets. The howler drove the thermostat into balmy regions. Eventually, the music in her ears mingled with the ringing bells of her alarm clock and she sat up, frozen. The howling ceased and the valley was back into the regular swing of winter.

"Got your sacrifice," Inge said, rubbing her cold arms.

The myth was that beasts from the mountain came down for a blood sacrifice, bringing with them the howling winds. A fun tale and no surprise that those gales carried a legend. Ignorance breeds fear and fascination. She'd never heard the scientific explanation behind the winds, but knew there had to be one. There is always an explanation. Likely, it was nothing more than volcanic send-off through a reedy gap in the rock, erupting in puffs, expelling temporary gales of heat. *Something.*

That morning, the valley was a thick sheet of ice. The regular frosty wind blew ice dust over the frozen surfaces. Igne arrived at her classroom to find a room with only half of the student body. The triplets sat at the back, the bright red glow gone from their skins. They wore the complexion of a full moon. So pale they appeared sickly, on the polar opposite spectrum from the day before.

The triplets wore short-sleeved blouses of a single design, differentiating in hue only. Their collective, cold gaze stared forward silently awaiting orders. Too good, more like robots than students.

"Androids," Inge whispered and put chalk to chalkboard. A history project, students' choice, work in groups of three.

For the morning, the class tackled assignments, goofing and working in nearly equal distribution. Igne treated the work time as she did most other days, the slim difference being that she veered toward the triplets more often. They looked a little better she thought, but she also wondered if it might be an adjustment in her mind.

"Lunchtime," Igne called.

The students leapt from their seats, brown bags crinkled, homemade fruit snacks became airborne. The triplets moved slowly toward their bags. Ericka fell forward and landed with a thump.

"Oh goodness!" Igne ran to her aid.

The standing sisters appeared awestruck, tears tumbling down over their sharp jaw lines. Igne turned the fallen girl onto her back. The sisters looked at one another and on point as always, they spoke a single word in unison, "Daddy," and sprinted from the classroom.

"Wake up, Ericka, wake up," Igne said. The girl was like a ragdoll in her arms, the students crowded in around them.

"I think that's Eisa," a boy said.

"No, Eila. Eisa wears the peach shirt," a girl said.

"Back up... Ericka wears the white shirt. Eisa the cream one. Eila the peach shirt," Igne said. It had taken time to get the color scheme right in her head. She couldn't tell the girls apart otherwise and sometimes they all wore white. Identical girls with pale blonde hair, pretty round faces, and standing four-feet even. Skinny. Usually speaking in accord, but only when directly addressed.

Ericka's eyes fluttered and Igne looked down at her expecting a recovery. It appeared a fainting spell, *but from what?* "Are you all right?"

Ericka nodded and attempted to sit forward. Igne gave her back a gentle nudge, eyes running along the smooth pale contours of the girl's arms. Scabby punctures bloomed bright red from the inner corners of her elbows.

"What are these from?"

The schoolhouse door burst open.

"Ericka," a deep voice said from atop a massive wide frame donning wolf fur clothing and a hat of goat hide. "Give me my girl." The man knelt over to scoop the weakened child.

"Are you her father?"

There was no response and Igne watched helplessly from the floor as the man carried away the child. The room fell into silence. Igne was down three more students.

"Was that Mr. Guild?" she asked.

"No, only the triplets are Guild. That's Mr. Hanna, but he's their dad. Never married the Guild mother and she died pushing out the triplets, so my ma says." Ivar was a fifteen-year-old standing nearly as tall as Hanna, though lacked the immensity.

"Hmm, well." Igne stood, brushed off the seat of her pants, and returned to her desk. "Still lunch for thirty minutes, if you're planning on going out, you'd best get a move."

Mouths smacked and paper bags ruffled and smoothed. Coats went from hooks to backs. It was a sweater weather day in the classroom. Igne noticed the three coats dangling four spots from her own hook and then thought again about the marks on Ericka's arms.

Those marks were odd. Too big for insulin, Igne's initial guess being that Ericka was diabetic. The mental wheels turned and she drafted a note to Mr. Hanna, requesting an interview, masquerading her concerns. She finished, and according to the clock, the kids had been on recess ten minutes longer than typical. She poked her head out the double doors. "Come on, come on!" She pulled the rope dangling below the large brass bell.

Rather than fight the oddity of the day, Igne and the children played games on the chalkboard. After class, Igne again looked to the coats still hanging near hers. She'd lost gumption. The girls would come to class without coats the following morning and she could deliver the note then.

Unfortunately, the triplets didn't show the following morning.

Nor the one after that.

There was no other choice then. She had to deliver the coats for the weekend. It was after four when she finally built the nerve necessary to walk over to the mysterious home on the eastern corner of the village.

For the month of January, Ravijk saw sunrise at ten in the morning and sundown at two in the afternoon. Being after four, it was black, aside from the sliver moon, and it was cold. The streets crunched and glittered shadowy white prismatic crystals under the slim silver glow. Mr. Hanna's home appeared to stretch long into the sky and Igne stepped into its shadow, knocked on the door, and listened for motion inside. There was a screeching of wooden chairs on wooden floors. Her heart jumped and she wanted to turn back, wanted to run and leave the coats in a heap.

Hanna answered the door. He was as impressive and foreboding as he had been during their first meeting. The lights from within the home cast an ominous glow, his aura in gold.

"Yes?" he asked, a curious turn of his head.

"I have coats," Igne managed to say, her legs weak. She had a brief vision of Hanna peeking around the street, seeing the emptiness, and dragging her inside, dining on her flesh, chomping on thigh meat as if torn from a chicken bone.

"From school, thank you." He took the heap from

Igne's arm. The coats seemed so insignificant under his hand, wrist curled like a hook or a J. The door began to close. Igne reached into her pocket and pulled out the sealed envelope.

"How are your girls?" She held out the envelope.

Hanna peered at this offering as if it had come from another galaxy.

He turned his head and yelled over his shoulder, "Girls!" The trio approached in a run. They all looked much healthier, proper color and moderate glow amid the shadowy atmosphere. He handed over the note.

"No, no, that's for you," Igne said. So badly, she wanted to run, but the best she could manage was to hinge her knees straight and avoid crumbling on the spot.

"Read it," the man ordered.

Igne wasn't certain which girl held the note thanks to a trick of light and shadows.

"It's really for you."

Hanna glowered. Igne shrank further, wishing it was possible to blow away, a snowflake on the breeze.

"Read it."

A small voice from inside began to speak, "Dear Mr. Hanna, I wanted to take this time to tell you what great students your girls have been. It's a real pleasure," the girl reading then paused, the letter was about to move into troublesome territory. "Um, oh, I lost my place. The girls are lots of fun and I hope they continue to be good."

Igne stared past the man. Her expression was curious and thankful. The note had been a bad idea and the triplets agreed.

The first reader stalled and another grabbed the sheet.

"I would also like to take this time to express concern," Igne gulped down glass shards of terror as the second reader began into the actual content, "that the girls could be doing more. With work, they could be the smartest kids ever. Thank you for your time, Ms. Dorthea."

Igne's heart played a thunder roll, but was slowing into something manageable. The girls hadn't read anything about the scabs, the peculiar behavior, or the general fear due to their blushing peculiarity.

The man's body eased. "So what? They need to read more? I can't help them, never learned, their mother was a smart one."

Igne's tongue twisted and stuck to the roof of her mouth. The wind whistled, she forced a smile, nodded, and turned. The entire universe seemed frozen, yet a hot island paradise when compared to the man behind her.

"They'll be back on Monday," he said.

The door closed and Igne moved on, in body, but not in mind. There was something off and the three young girls knew it.

It took time to get along in a new town. Igne hadn't yet worked her way into any social groups. Not that many existed, most of the people in Ravijk are there because that's where they are, it's who they are, birth to death. The town survives on a barter system, work for food, food for food, and so on. Igne was one of only a few wage-earning citizens.

The money she spent in the community trickled down and out for foreign items. Lumber and grains mostly, but also into the entertainment sector.

Townsfolk met at the hall to watch the communal satellite dish, drink beer, eat soup and fresh bread, and to learn of civilizations beyond the valley walls. Rather than take a seat in the darkened room before the television with the majority, she took a stool at the bar. There was a reddish light, a soft ambience clouding over two wide-framed men and a chubby woman. Each held a chunky ceramic mug that remained cool for hours.

Igne ordered a beer and leaned toward the chubby woman, the woman turned and revealed a smile of more dark than light. A common picture as there was no dentist in the valley and no conceptions about oral hygiene.

"You're the teacher," the woman said.

Igne nodded and grinned.

"Nice to meet you. I'm Mags, that's Leif, and that's Par." Mags pointed down the bar to the men, they appeared to be twins.

Igne offered her name and then listened as the twins told stories of everyone that entered or left the hall. The bartender, a man with scruffy white hair covering most of his head and jaw, much like a lion's mane, refilled the cups as they emptied. The men and the woman sounded sufficiently soused to ask questions of and to expect candid responses from.

The topic was Hanna. The trio grew silent. The twins appeared sullen. They finished their drinks, eyeing Igne, slamming the mugs on the bar, and stomping out of the hall.

"What did I say?"

"Oh, it isn't your fault. Leif and Par miss their brother. They lived with Mr. Hanna's father, maybe grandfather, I can't recall. Had their childhoods in that place until their brother Randolph died. Old Hanna believed in the myth, made the boys spill blood during the Howl, put three bowls out the back door. Come morning, the Howl was done and the blood was gone. Wolves drink blood, it's like champagne to them," Mags said.

"Must've been hard, what happened to Hanna's father, or grandfather, or…?"

"Died I reckon. Nobody ever saw him again, but there's always at least one Hanna in the place. The boys moved out after their brother died."

"They were triplets?" The mathematical unlikelihood in such a small sample size was something special.

"Yes, the Hanna blood's good for triplets."

"So how did Rudolph die?"

"Randolph," Mags corrected. "Story is, he froze to death waiting after a Howler left off, but that's just talk. Nobody knows for sure. Though some say he failed to offer sacrifice." Mags wore a sly grin and left without another word.

Igne finished her mug and returned home to muse. The scabs, the past, Hanna's father, it all mashed, and Igne was certain the man was letting the girls' blood to sacrifice to the wind.

"It's insane."

She'd spent the weekend playing different scenarios in her mindscape as to how she'd get answers from the girls and save them from their father. Heroic teacher fantasies.

On Monday morning, the temperature shifted downwards to forty-three below. It hurt to breathe. Lungs threatened to shatter like hollow ice. Nostril hairs became frosty blocks and eyelids clung as the moisture at the edges solidified.

Five students braved the weather. There were two teens near the front, a lovey-dovey pair willing to face anything for the heart, and at the back of the room were the triplets. The girls stared forward and the two teens stared into each other's eyes. It was sweet and utterly ridiculous.

"Well, I can't do much with these numbers," Igne said. "How about we do story time?"

Nobody answered.

Although long due for an upgrade, the cassette deck continued spinning every time called upon, wheels creaking, speakers crackling. The class listened, most had read the homey classics, Gunnarsson, Ibsen,

Andersen, and saw it a treat to listen of the world beyond their reach, in both time and space. A soft mannish voice announced the unabridged version of *The Idiot*, translated from Russian. It was the longest of any of the audio books in the school's collection, twenty-two ninety-minute cassettes.

Igne sat at her desk, mindlessly shuffling papers, glancing up now and then to catch the teens stealing kisses while the triplets kept eyes forward. "Knock it off or I'll tell your mothers," Igne said, the teens split, their chair legs squeaking as they parted.

Igne walked past them, offering a grave glance, and knelt to talk to the triplets. They all wore white. Impossibly similar. Replicas of one another.

Before she could speak, one of the girls whispered, "Ms. Dorthea, can we do our project on the Howl? On Ravijk Valley?"

It wasn't how she'd expected to fall onto the topic. She'd almost forgotten about the project. Most children choose Egypt or Rome for their history project, as there's an abundance of information available and a Hollywood richness beyond the more reliable library books.

"What do you mean?"

"We want to do a report about the myths and what people do," one of the triplets said.

"Yeah," the other two agreed.

"Okay." Igne hunkered lower and leaned in, the girls all smelled of minty bar soap. "Girls, does your father hurt you?"

Eyes bulged and the girls gazed forward, non-answering. Their unwillingness to speak an answer of its own.

"You know, whatever he does, he shouldn't. This is the modern world." The sentence came out of her mouth like morning breath. It wasn't the modern world, everywhere else, maybe, but not in the secluded valley. "He can't do things to you and get away with it."

The encouragement did nothing. The girls were rocks. Igne gave up for the time and moved back to her desk to listen about the naïve *Prince Myshkin*.

Igne sent the students home before sundown. It was better than ten degrees warmer than it was that morning, but the window for the balmy minus-thirty centigrade was a small one.

Igne spent the evening and night fretting over the idea that the triplets faced real danger. How does one harm his own children? How does one still believe in such nonsense?

The weather had warmed to numbers that were more comfortable. The following morning, the class returned from hibernation. Igne hadn't heard another peep from the Guild girls and her conversation attempts went nowhere. Days became weeks, Igne couldn't let it go, and finally the pre-Howl came.

The triplets lined the back of the classroom, their faces aglow, red, the heat emanated from their bodies as if fires burned in their bellies. The ideas spun, they were like that last time before Ericka fell ill with scabby tracks about her arms. Igne watched them closely. They sat, heads swaying, drinking water from bottles, eating only dried elk hunks at lunch.

"I'll see you all tomorrow," Igne said.

The girls burst forward showing their first spurts of energy all day. Eisa dropped two pages onto Igne's desk before she passed the stalled students hoping to avoid contact with the girls.

Something had changed from the weeks prior. The two lovey-dovey students no longer held hands or made kissy-faces. Instead, the boy had a new girl. A girl one year younger. It didn't sit well with the foregone love. Claws came out. Taut under pressure, screams emitted from both sides, scalps withstanding tremendous strain from yanked strands. Right then, Igne forgot about the triplets and focussed on the warring girls.

She separated them, seated them, sent lover-boy away, and called homes on the bulky rotary phone on the wall behind her desk. Mothers laughed, fathers shook their heads. The entire hubbub took an hour. Alone in her classroom, Igne finally picked up the report from her desk, just as the Howl began.

She read and reread and again. This was a detailed report of bloodletting and of appeasing mountain beasts. Beasts with voices like banshees, bodies of men, heads like goats, and hands of burning steel. The report explained everything their father told them, the book where he showed drawings of the beasts, of the things he believed real, promised eventual, great sacrifices, ones that repeated and drew back into the forevers of time. Someday, one of the girls would die for the sake of the village. It always was and would be.

"My goodness," Igne spoke without hearing her voice over the winds. She dropped the sheet to her desk, considered the chances of success, took her parka, and ran from the room.

A dark wall of hot air blew into her face, screaming as it went. It thumped into her ears and came directly from the east, from almost right behind Hanna's home. Her body angled against the wind, pushing through the invisible force. She'd never stayed out during a Howl and never noticed the subtle scents carried within. It was metallic, sour, and familiar, yet difficult to place.

The short walk took nearly twenty minutes. Sweat dripped down Igne's face and slid along her arms and legs beneath her heavy coat. Her hair was a drenched mat and she felt as if she'd run a marathon. Exhausted, sore, and greedy for finish.

She pounded on the door. No answer. She pounded

harder, catching her breath as the house sheltered against the gale force winds.

"Let me in!"

Turning the handle, the door opened. The air inside was twice as hot. She neither saw nor heard anyone. The written report described basement cells with cots, and archaic needles and glass tubing that ran from their veins into copper urns. What they hadn't described was the main floor or where to find the basement entry.

She discovered the kitchen beyond the dining area, no door. She found the living room and a den of sorts. There was a door leading upstairs to what she assumed were bedrooms. The home was massive and dark, many of the light bulbs were decades old, glowing orangey yellows rather than bluish whites. She found the pantry and a door with several open padlocks and locked bolts.

She tugged, shouting in chorus with the Howling outside. She looked about the pantry, for something to breakdown the door, something that might master the locks. As she turned, a thump blackened her sight and the last vision she had was of seven-foot goat.

Igne awoke under bulbous ivory bulbs dangling from the ceiling. Her body slumped against a wall. A few feet away, three tight cells with heavy steel bars and the imprisoned girls. The glassy lines ran red with blood. The giant goat, or rather Mr. Hanna donning animal hides, worked on Eisa's arm, removing a fat needle.

It was much cooler in the basement. The room was long, walls of stone and steel, at the far end, away from Hanna, away from the girls, the cells and their running blood, there was a dusty workbench cluttered with tools. Spider webs draped lazily like tossed quilts long in years but short in remaining threads.

Igne crawled, quietly, the din outside muffled by the home's foundation and yet still offered enough noise to cover the drag of her boots against the floor. Aching all over, but mostly behind her eyes, through the top of her skull, and into her brain, she tasted the familiar scent. It was blood. Blood from inside, blood that never met the surface to mingle with the other scents of the world. Pure, untainted blood. An essence in bloom.

Igne swallowed a helping of deep red fluid and reached through the thick webs. Fat, furry-bodied spiders burst into action at the motion, scurrying onto her hand and up the sleeve of her coat before she had a chance to pull her arm away. She stifled a scream as she felt them inside her parka. She dropped the jacket and swatted frantically, knocking two spiders from her arms, unnoticing of the eight-legged monster nesting in her damp hair.

She grabbed a heavy wooden block hammer. Hanna had moved onto Ericka, closing her puncture. Igne saw her chance and swung back, her body screaming in agony from the knock to her head. Hanna turned at the last second and threw out an arm. He blocked the hammer, but his bones cracked and splintered in unnatural directions. Inge swung again. Hanna grimaced, dodged the strike and slammed his fist into Igne's nose. The soft layer of cartridge and bone burst into a fat red smear like a stomped grape.

The battered teacher slid backwards and Hanna returned his attention, finally getting to Eila's arm, the blood spilled over the lip of the copper urn.

The spider riding Igne's head dug into her scalp where she sat. The pain was horrid, but awakening. She scrambled to her knees and took to crawling. The hammer seemed years away, her eyes remained glued on the wide back of the enormous man. A spider ran along the floor and to Hanna's boot, up his back, and onto his arm.

"What are you doing over here?" he asked, lifting the limb, the wide bone jutting jagged beneath the furs of his parka.

He turned in time to see the hammer's block swipe across his jaw, cracking and separating with a heavy wet thud. His conscious gone long before three of his spat teeth landed. He toppled and flattened the spider.

"Girls, girls!" Igne said, slumping and lurching toward the cells. The girls leaned forward, weak and drained. The beleaguered woman tapped and fingered around Hanna's body, feeling for pockets, looking for the hard edges of keys.

"The wall," Ericka said from the central cell before she fell back, lightheaded.

Putting the pain aside, Igne dragged her unwilling body across the room. The keys dangled from a jutting nail. They were long iron keys, archaic with two rabbit's teeth dipping from the shaft. The cells used the same key, the girls sat slowly, unable to move with the urgency necessary.

Ericka and Eisa leaned against their swinging cell doors.

"Get up, come on." Igne helped Eila, kicking over the copper urn dripping red next to the girl's bed.

"I'm so tired," she whispered, leaning, sapping much of Igne's energy.

They pushed on toward the door. Locked. Igne panicked for a second before the remembrance of the keys blared something like an eye roll at her panic. The door opened with a heavy click.

Dark enveloped the light, devouring it as the steps began ascent. Into the blackness of the staircase they moved, dragging feet, kicking each step and moving with slow nervous motion. They leaned on the walls, raising and dipping with fat rounded surfaces. It was as if plaster were pregnant, or if the original builder dropped stones into wet cement.

"What's on the walls?" Igne asked. The report hadn't

described the walls.

None answered the question. The dips were sharp at times, Igne found her fingers travelling below the surface layers at others. The Howl grew louder with every step and was the only promise that they moved in the correct direction at all. Igne almost fell backwards when she finally reached the door, bumping her agonised head, sending a shockwave through her system. She felt for a handle, the girls pushed up against the harrowed woman.

"Stop, stop!" Igne said.

Nobody heard. The door handle spun but the door remained locked, she found a keyhole, blind fingering. A key slid inside, too loose. A shove from behind pushed her hard against the door.

"Back!"

The next key entered the door, the locked clicked, and they all fell forward, looking back to see Hanna groping along the wall from below and his bloodied face hanging loosely like a rubber half-mask.

The light offered more information.

The walls were of decayed flesh and aged bones, the rounded dips and craters, skulls, ribs, pelvic regions devoid of life, though brimming with horror.

Igne screamed, understanding the bones and dried leather skin. Every bone matched a sacrificial child. And so many she'd touched just now, running her pained head and tired hands against their surfaces.

Hanna carried two urns of blood, slowing his chase to a crawl. The triplets stumbled behind Igne who bore a new energy, anything to escape the stairway walls. She staggered, woozy and flailing. The front door seemed miles away. They plodded, howling out in anguish, crying along with the winds. Once outside, Igne glanced back. Hanna no longer followed.

He couldn't be far. Igne knew it and she forced her

distressed frame on and out into the blackness of Ravijk. Lights shone from living room windows like lighthouse beacons, promising safety on the shore. Safety from a violent and insane father. Safety from a man living in a myth.

The Howl assisted their motion, a heavy hand moving them along their path. The closest home had light. Igne led the way. Trudging hand-in-hand, Eila dragged down on both arms. Igne and Ericka gripped tighter.

Fists slammed on the neighbour's door, a face came to the window, and the light inside died.

"Please!" Igne moved away, watching as the lights next door dim.

She pulled the girls further, she wasn't certain she could make it all the way home, but she had to try. As they pushed on, every potential saviour turned down their lights as if apologizing in advance.

On her scalp, the nesting spider felt pangs of homesickness.

Not halfway to her cottage, Igne stopped with an agony that she'd never known riding atop her head. Deeper and deeper the spider burrowed. It felt like acid burning just behind her flesh. She fell, grasping her scalp, hair coming away in clumps. The spider beneath her skin continued its search, digging for peace, frantic for its nest.

Igne clawed her face, screaming as the spider dug out through her nose. The freed creature ran confusedly until the winds collected it and the Howl launched it tumbling away from its base and arachnid family.

Igne's sinus oozed black poison. She blinked away blobs of ink pouring forth from her eyes like Texas crude tears. Hot blood dripped down her throat.

Disoriented, the triplets attempted to stand her up. Their teacher's head doubling and then tripling in size, bloated with intrusive poison secreted by the long gone interloper as it cut paths behind the once pretty face.

Eisa shook Ericka as Ericka shook Igne who'd fallen back to the wet street. "Gone, she's gone!" Eisa screamed, pointing back to where Eila once stood. There was not a trace.

Ericka's fingers slipped from Eisa's and Eisa peered about her. Gone, both of her sisters, gone. Only she and the teacher remained. Eisa hugged onto Igne, if the Howlers should come for her, she would not go alone.

~

The winds ceased for a sixth time since the last proper sacrifice. Hanna looked out onto the yard he'd known for more than two thousand years, gazing over the homes, the dwellings of the scared. Any one of them could be next. Missing the sacrifice doomed the town until he replenished the source: Guild blood.

He shook thinking that he'd spilled Ericka's urn in his rush and had managed to get only Eisa's outside. He loved every child of the Guild he'd raised. It hurt so much to lose them.

The Howl would take its sacrifice. Hanna fought against tears. A single drop betrayed his will.

"Supper, supper, where are you?" The voice whistled a hollow tune behind the words.

Hanna turned to the speaker. "In here, I'm coming." He wiped his eye.

The hungry faces of the beasts lingered in his head. One had received sacrifice, the other two ate the source of the flow, drinking the well, flesh, bone, and breath.

Hanna walked to the kitchen. He smelled potatoes, goat, and the new Guild mother.

Already feeling huge, Igne held a palm at the small of her back. She hadn't seriously considered having children, not yet. It was a miracle after that night. She'd been bitten by a spider, had a fever dream, and imagined a set of triplets.

Leaving her post at the school was wise. Hanna agreed. Staying would only feed her delusions about triplets and the mountain winds. Besides, her deformity scared the students and she didn't want to scare anybody.

Hanna kissed Igne's bulbous, darkened, hairless brow. She was pregnant with triplets. He'd be a father again. Igne would die giving birth, as it is and always shall be. Until then, the beasts of the Howl would cry and eat of the village, ceasing only once the agreed sacrifice resumed.

Of the Knoll

Always follow the rules. Follow the rules and everything will go as planned. Everyone will have a good time and everyone will be safe.

There's always one and he's—it's almost always a *he*—is never the one that gets hurt. He always has that stupid look on his face when things go wrong, colorless and insipid. It's as if the idea that rules are there for a reason never occurs to him, as if the rules are there to give boys something to moan over and eventually break.

There was a snap overhead, a series of small cracks, and finally the swooping whoosh of an accident hungry for lives. The straw on the floor soaked much of the blood, but enough splattered like an abattoir kill room, freckling the ancient wood like a miscoloured Dalmatian. Jacob and Ronan ran as fast as their coveralls permitted. It took only an instant to see what had happened and to understand it fully. That rotten troublemaker Justin still held the rope. The rope that led to the pulley, the pulley that had but one rule of its own: don't over-bind. The rope sat three times over its limit.

Justin had that wishy-washy expression, the color drained from his cheeks, mouth agape, that guilty look.

"Quickly!" Jacob yelled and then added as an afterthought, "Mother, call Mother, now!"

Justin backed away from the bodies. It was horrid, but it didn't feel like his fault. He didn't even want to go on the boring old vacation.

His mom and two other women lay on the floor, his mom's arm missing all of its flesh from where the snapped beam swung into her. It peeled her, but it wasn't an arm wound that might put her out permanently. That beam connected somewhere in her chest. That was worse.

Justin heard the wind leave her lungs in a hurry, right after the first snap. A couple creaks and a whipping later, another beam came down and smacked into the others. Their bodies jerked backward like a pair of Rock'em Sock'em Robots. There was blood. There were brains.

Here was a trio on death's doorstep and here was a boy with a rope.

Justin's father, Rory, chased the yells and found his son inside the barn. Three men and an old woman stood over the body of his wife. Justin ran to him.

"What did you do?" Rory said in a stern angry father kind of way.

Justin couldn't answer. He wanted to cry. When he was younger, he cried away so many punishments. Somewhere recently, along life's road, his well dried and he had to face his mistakes. But it wasn't his fault. He only wanted to see how much rope would go 'round. How would he know that the pulley was more than three-hundred years old? Why did they still use it if it was fragile?

"Bring me my things and," the old woman said— Mother of Naket Knoll—and pointed a knobby finger to the visitors, "take them away. This ain't for outsider eyes."

Justin and Rory didn't argue.

"Can't we call an ambulance, Dad?" Justin asked.

"Ambulance can't get in here. How come you can't be a good son?" Rory spoke without emotion and in a matter-of-fact tone. "How come, Justin?"

Justin went through a number of excuses, but something about the severity of the situation demanded that he at least feign remorse. "I don't know. I guess I'm bad."

Time isn't a real thing. Anybody waiting on the outside while a loved one went through a procedure on the inside can tell you that. Those seconds aren't seconds, they're hours, awful agonizing hours. Nothing else exists. It was only minutes earlier when Rory thought he could give it all up and move to a place like Naket Knoll, that these people had it right.

He, Justin, and Juliette, his wife, lived in the go, go, go goddamn-you world of Vancouver and it left him ragged and the weekends were short. The birds, the trees, the fields, it was the sun that really did it to him. Sometimes it seemed like months would pass before the sun showed its face in Vancouver, but in Naket Knoll, it was always sunny unless it was night and at night, it rained, not a lot, but enough.

The crops flourished, everything flourished. Smiles, health, vibrancy, everything flourished.

The sun started to fall faster and the one thousand years Rory stood waiting outside the barn came to an end. The men carried Juliette, wrapped in a cotton cocoon, toward the main house. Mother's house. There was little blood and Rory wondered if he hadn't imagined that the accident wasn't a great deal worse than it was. Mother stepped out and reality set back the truth. She was bloody as Carrie White's bar soap.

"Are they going to make it?" Rory asked, but what he meant was, *is my wife going to live, I don't give a crapola about the others, is my wife going to make it?*

"Only time will answer something like that," Mother said with a soft voice. She then turned her focus toward Justin and hardened. "You don't go in my barn and you don't go near my shed."

Time, what did they know about time? Since choosing the hill in that wooded little valley, they hadn't changed much, not how civilized time dictated. Sure, they still died, no beating time on that one, but they ignored the modern world, it was as if they'd just stepped off their wagons and set to settling, forever. The only thing that changed since that first crop was the small needs. This, no doubt, happened when a visitor soiled the village with information and exotic treats: coffee and sugar, Swiss chocolate, curry, mangos, pears, lemons, Average Joe-Household mainstays. For any of it, they needed money and for money, you had to interact with that civilized world following time's rules of progress.

Starting twenty-years earlier, they took in visitors, a vacation setting unlike any other. Sure, there are farm retreats all over the world where you worked your butt off rather than relaxed, and Naket Knoll demanded effort there was no arguing that, but it was the other things that made the place different.

If you went to Naket Knoll, you had to learn the old ways, the ways of the sun god, the moon god, the earth god, the fire god, and the water god. It seemed a little odd at first. Though was it so strange? People prayed to the moon and sun long before anyone nailed a skinny man with a complex to a cross. Even longer before Muhammed whipped up a script and took over an army.

There were no rich people, no poor people, all started on an equal basis, all had to prove their value, a significance impossible to inherit at birth. The value of humanity according to the land they hoped to dwell upon.

It was a better way, electricity added stress in the long view. It seems so great to flick a switch and get light, it seems even better to finish your day's plowing in only hours rather than days, but it always catches. The more energy destroyed, pulled from the earth, from the sky, the less life becomes about living and more about sitting and counting minutes before retirement or death.

Rory played with the idea of living a life like that. He even mentioned it, half-jokingly to test Juliette's reaction, in passing, with an off-handed suggestion that life would be pretty nice in a place like Naket Knoll.

She'd agreed.

That was then.

He didn't want to be there anymore. He wanted his wife in a hospital with lights and beeping and nurses and drugs and folks in blue gowns and masks. A helicopter could land in the village, somewhere, but they'd never get a message to come. Cell phones lost signal hours away from where they were. Even the delivery truck that brought the coffee and the other goods went only as far as the end of the road, more than nine kilometers of uneven hiking trail.

Juliette was there to stay until she got better or until she died.

Both Rory and Justin went off to beds in their tiny private rooms. Rory looked across the hall from the room he and Juliette shared to the room that the other injured women had shared. It was a bit of a surprise to him when the old-fashioned rules of Naket Knoll said nothing about same-sex couples, but the more he thought about it, the more it made sense. The major religions made prominent feature of self-denial and abolishing freedoms, these village folk followed a religion that didn't make mention of sex at all.

He stared at the open door to the empty room and wondered if his son might be responsible for someone's death, possibly three deaths. As a father, part of that was his guilt to live with.

He shook away the thought and lied down on his double bed. Over the twenty-one years of marriage, no matter the mattress beneath, he'd missed only a dozen or so nights away from his wife's sleeping, snoring, farting side.

"She isn't dying."

He so badly wanted to sleep, let the time pass without notice, bring an end to the mystery, life or death, time it would take, so said Mother. She would know. She'd defied time up to that point.

Ninety-one, think I'm fibbing? Where's a tale like that bound to fetch me? No sir, no lie, I been around a long time. Seen the seasons pass a good bundle and plan on a bundle more.

She didn't look older than seventy-five. A bit like a raisin, a pale white raisin, but her eyes showed a sharp cognition and she spoke, although with a happy-bumpkin vocabulary, in wise and strangely prophetic bursts of information. Mother was also the only person capable of offering any kind of medical advice or assistance.

When I'm ready, I'll spill my knowhow to the next in line, she'd said when Justin prodded her about her age. *I'll not go yet, according to the willows and the river. They gave me a little show, I got more than a lil' while a kicking left in these old bones. The wind's gonna send me a new trainee soon, I reckon, takes time to learn what I knows.*

Justin made that smartass face that went right along with his smartass tone, chips and dip, cookies and milk, peas and carrots. He began a mocking rebuttal, but

Mother took his hand and his eyes bugged. Juliette and Rory watched this in a state of suspended horror. They couldn't really control their son and hoped the old woman had a sense of humor.

Mother hummed and chanted for about twenty-seconds, eyes closed, body shaking, and then she stopped, opened an eye and smiled. *Guess you's right, I'm just a crazy old bird. I wouldn't take too many plane rides if I was you, then again if I was you, I wouldn't take no plane rides.* The laughter was high, almost a witchy cackle.

Justin snapped his hand away.

Things were more normal after that. Rory and Justin worked much of the time rotating between the kitchen and the field, whereas Juliette worked in the barn. The horses chose who worked with them on a sliding rejection scale. Justin wasn't to go into the barn. The residents couldn't explain why the horses didn't like him. He didn't mind at all.

There was also pigs in the barn and their manure made his eyes water.

Justin went in only once and that's when what happened, happened.

In bed, mulling it over, Rory raked his fingers over his temples. It was hard to breathe beneath such new pressure.

~

Jody sat up, barely, with great effort. Her head ached and throbbed while her entire body pulsed, her blood seemed thick and gritty within her veins. "But I'm alive," she attempted to say, spewing but a viscous muttering of tinny tasting saliva between her lips. The memory came to her in a hot red flood of pain.

She blinked, only the gentle flicker of a candle outside the room danced, leaving nothing to see. She blinked again and the memory furthered along its ugly trail. It was all there, that boy, the blood, her Dini.

"Dini," she moaned, her lips rough and awful.

"Shh now, child," Mother's soothing voice said as she approached with the flickering candle. She sat to Jody's side on a small chair. Next to the bed was a night table and on that night table was a bowl of liquid.

"Dini," Jody whispered.

"Now when I say quiet, I means it, so zip it. Your girl gonna be fine, she took a knocking like you did. Maybe a little worse, but I patched her and I patched you. You rest and soon enough you'll be up and about and so will Dini, but first you got to shush." Mother rung out a cloth into the bowl and began wiping Jody's head, neck, and face.

It stank, but a familiar not so bad kind of smell. Still, not so great. Jody inhaled deeply through her nose as the cloth passed over her dry lip. It was like old beer, warm and yeasty.

"Now, I'm gonna leave you and I expect you to rest. No more worrying about your lady. I'll get her right as sun, right as the moon, right as the corn and the rye, and the beans and hay fields, she'll be right and so will you, but you gotta rest to heal." Mother pulled a little pouch from her pocket and sprinkled a dusty substance from within over the flickering flame. The flame jumped and grabbed at the granules, glowing purple. Another scent entered Jody's nostrils. Before she could place it, her eyelids snapped shut.

Mother stood and looked down at the poor girl, wrapped and stained with old blood. Jody was the best of the three. Juliette wasn't much worse, but a bit worse, and Dini lay barely clinging after a brief tug of war with Death himself.

Death always wins in the end, but you can beat him for a time.

Dini hadn't stirred and Mother suspected she

wouldn't.

Mother pocketed her pouch and stepped into the hallway with the candle, burning on its weathered wooden mantle. It was bedtime, well past by most folk's standards. Mother hadn't slept more than four or five hours a night for the last year. She was worried that her apprentice was a no-show, and time was running out.

Silliness, now she knew better than to worry. Knew it all along, but her apprentice had come, surely.

A cough shifted her attention and her destination. *No rest for this winter chicken,* she thought and laughed at the idea that she was any kind of chick, *not for a coon's age, not for a coon's great granddaddy's age*. She chuckled a little more.

The cough barked again.

"I'm coming, don't get your knickers twisted."

Mother followed the sound into Juliette's room where the woman lay. Her face was purple and bumpy, her chest no better as it heaved up and down. An incision rose with her breaths, threatening to tear, the wiry grainy threads holding her together at about their limits. Mother pulled a small glass jar from her pocket. A dry golden-yellow paste inside, Mother spit two big gobs of saliva and phlegm into the mix, recapped, and shook. The golden-yellow paste became a glue-like substance and she poured it over the incision. Holding the candle closer to inspect, she saw as she hoped when the threads thickened and strengthened.

"That'll do fine."

Juliette's eyes remained closed, but she continued coughing, and with every cough, the incision threatened to expose her insides. Rustling through the pockets of her apron and then her dress, she finally found what she sought. She set the candle on a small desk next to the bed and worked away with miniature pestle and mortar. She crushed a bit from her pouch and a bit from her breast pocket, corn kernel, grains of oat and rye, two pine needles, and orange soil from the southern shore of the river. She spat into the mix and churned it further. She spat again and again until the liquid was light and easy like watered-down syrup.

With one hand behind Juliette's upper back and the other tipping the mortar to her patient's lips, Mother fed the liquid until it was gone. After a few minutes of quiet, not even a heavy breath came from the tender chest. The old woman went off to bed.

"Tomorrow gone be as hard as the last, I reckon." She blew out the candle flame.

~

Rory woke after eight, missing the numerous rooster calls and the breakfast bell. Although never having given much weight to a god, he said a little prayer for his wife, directed to any open ears in the heavens above.

Life was so easy at Naket Knoll, even clinging to worry and misery didn't take him to the spot that so many visit during times of anguish and despair. It was impossible to sit and wait, that was the worst option. He walked to the little washroom at the end of the building. An overhead system built outside allowed gravity to work its magic. The water was sunshine warmed. Rory opened the faucet and splashed his face.

The shower ran down a polished wooden sink and outside, into a deep hole. He spread some toothpaste over his Oral B and worked the motions. A small rash, red and itchy, had broken around his armpits. When he first arrived, he wanted to embrace everything about the place, natural deodorant included. The white gritty powder ribbed into the skin and, to his surprise, worked almost as well as Old Spice.

Something in the deodorant didn't agree with him and he made the switch back to the blue stuff in the red capsule.

There were three living quarters in Naket Knoll, one was exclusive to visitors, another to a handful of families, and the final belonged to the singles. Mother had her own lodge and it doubled as the hospital with its three additional rooms aside from the main bedroom. Mother lived in that home for more years than she dared remember. She'd outlived all of her children, only a few grandbabies still ran around the property. The direct descendants of Mother were becoming rare.

Naket Knoll isn't for everyone, isn't for most. When people left to see the world, they rarely came back.

It was hot and sunny already. Both aspects went to the wayside of Rory's attention. He didn't notice the sweet smell of clean nature. He didn't notice the distant sounds of busy men and women pulling on the same rope, working to the same goal. He didn't care anymore.

He walked into the dining hall. A piece of him wished to go, leave Juliette's broken body and the boy behind, forget this pain. It was too much. The scent of pancakes and clear syrup entered his nose. It did nothing for his mood.

With only a mug of coffee, Rory sat in the busy room. The people of Naket Knoll worked hard and they enjoyed breakfast. It was rare that they spent less than an hour and a half sitting, discussing the fields, the trees, the sun, their children, the animals, everything about their tiny world. On that morning, they spoke of nothing but of the accident. Rory sat alone at a rectangular table suitable for eight plates. Men and women walked past him, muttering nice words and touching his shoulders with gentle hands.

A plate of two pancakes with syrup and butter landed on the table in front of him. "Gotta eat if you plan to work today," Mother said. "Of course, I can't force ya, but a day's work has a way of putting time in the past."

"I was thinking maybe I'd take the day off," Rory

said feeling strangely guilty about it.

"Like I said, can't force ya, but it's good to work, the harder you work the easier the day, and come moon-side-up, your lids will be so darn heavy only your pillow will trouble you, won't be energy left to fret."

Rory thought about it and decided she probably knew tragedy better than he did. "All right." The heavy cakes went down.

~

Justin entered the dining hall and walked toward his father, Mother intercepted him a few feet prior to contact with the man. "You gonna be a busy beaver today, boy."

"What?" Justin he couldn't believe the yokel dared say something like that after what had happened. Didn't she understand he had to go home, get away from the slow world?

"Hard work will help you get over your grief," she said and then leaned in to whisper, "Not that I reckon you got any grief at all, but don't you worry, you'll not work to forget like your dad. No boy, you'll work 'cause I can see by looking at your skinny arms and weak legs, you don't care for work. You'll know punishment. You'll work 'cause it hurts you."

Justin looked over the woman's shoulder. Rory bused his dish and headed to the door. He tried to follow his father, push past the old woman, but she stood solid.

"Out of my way lady, or I'll tell my dad and we'll sue you."

Mother stifled a laugh. "Sue me for what, boy? You gonna see a change I reckon, real soon, you gonna see a change. Your mama and your daddy, they already started the change and you kicked it into gear yourself. I suggest you do what you're told."

Horace, a massive blonde man approached Justin from behind and pulled his arm. Justin attempted to fight the hold, screaming obscenities and scratching at the man's fingers. It wasn't something Horace saw necessary to put up with, not from that boy. He wound and clocked Justin in the chin.

The room darkened as he crumpled. There was nothing else to moan over, not until he awoke anyway.

Rory had watched it all, envious, the boy was bad and the giant blonde had a nerve that he didn't.

Outside the dining hall, Roderick leaned against a wall smoking tobacco from a corncob pipe. "If it makes you feel better, I think Mother fixed your wife up, only trouble now gonna have to pass some time."

"I don't know what I'll do if you're wrong," Rory said. That was true. Life would not be life without Juliette.

"Understood." Roderick tapped free the ash and ember from his pipe. He motioned for Rory to follow. The men walked without word. The first stop was to a small tool shed. Roderick handed out chisels, a pickaxe, a hammer, a sledgehammer, and a rope net.

It was a daily mystery what work entailed from one morning to the next. Roderick led beyond the field path and toward the river. The sun blazed hot and promised nothing but hotter. However, it was nice in the shade.

They stopped in front of a short natural wall of granite jutting from the earth three feet that ran for about twenty lengthways. "Some of the stones in the stove pit took frost and cracked over the winter. We need four new ones."

Rory was useless wielding a sledgehammer. Roderick laughed and encouraged him, taking the hammer now and then to show a proper form and angle.

A hunk of stone dropped from the wall. "Not a bad size, but gonna take some time to fit it," Roderick said. "Easier work anyway. Give you a wee rest from the sledge."

The sweat dripped and ran about Rory's body, he was soaked and it was as if they'd only been out for minutes, perhaps an hour. With chisel in hand, Roderick showed Rory how to snap away bits of stone without breaking his back.

"You try," Roderick said.

Rory took the chisel and hammer, clinked once, steel on granite, before off in the distance the lunch bell called everyone in. "Couldn't be," he said and looked at his watch, and sure enough, it was after one.

"We'll have to work a little faster after lunch." Roderick smiled.

They went in and rushed back out. Hours flew by. The men smashed and chipped, sweated and sang. Information filtered into Naket Knoll naturally and the good things seemed to stick. Although they lacked an essential piece to enjoying topical hit music in its hay-day, they managed to piece together songs from the lips of visitors, the lips of the deliverymen, the lips on the other side of the deliverymen's radio, and then created any missing pieces.

Roderick had a thing for an album that came north with a particularly crude teenager some decades earlier. The boy and his boom box were gone, but Roderick kept the music, in a manner.

"*To live and die in Naket Knoll, it's the place to be,*" Roderick sang, "*you got to be here to know it…*" And then rapped beyond the hook, "*It's a bush of angels and little danger, life outside the Knoll couldn't be more stranger.*"

Rory laughed. "That's good, I know it, but don't. What is it?"

"Tupac, Knoll-style." Roderick grinned wide, proud of his adlibbing.

Roderick continued his personal remix of *To Live & Die in L.A.* until his words muddled and flowed without break into David Bowie's *Space Oddity*. Rory joined in, familiar with rock, because everybody knows Bowie at one level or another.

The supper bell sounded promptly at seven. Roderick and Rory bagged the stones and dragged them up the hard packed dirt path toward the stove pit.

Mother approached the men as they set out to replace the tools. "After supper, you can visit in on Juliette, if you'd like."

"Is she up? Is she awake?" Rory shouted, unable to control his emotion.

"In and out. I think it would be good for her to rest, but just as good for you to see her. The mind is a harder fix than the body. You eat and wash first, don't need no infection."

"Right, right, I'll go wash and then…"

"Then you gonna eat some supper, don't need ya falling over, neither. She and the others are fixing up in the Mother house, right down the hall from me so I can keep an eye. So after supper, you go on in, her door'll be open."

"Right, right." Rory was giddy as a child, but frowned suddenly. "Where's the boy?"

"He's in waiting to feast, was the first one to the table. I don't doubt he grew him some blisters today. Horace has a way about getting a boy to pull his heft."

"Good, good," Rory said and then he and Roderick raced off to the men's shower.

He missed pressure, but the warm water that trickled did the job. Three men besides Rory and Roderick showered in the circular room, almost cheek-to-cheek, all too hungry to wait until later and it was against the rules to sully the dinner table with the day's work. Unlike lunch, supper was a sacred meal.

Rory dressed, followed closely by the other men, and joined those waiting in the dining hall. Justin ran to his father when he saw him. "That man," he pointed a finger at Horace, "hit me, he can't do that." Justin was frantic.

"You're lucky I don't hit you, there's going to be some changes when we get home, Justin. Big changes."

Justin looked at his father with disgust in his eyes. "Whatever, I'll tell them what you said. Then I'll call Children's Aid—"

"Dial all you want, your phone won't work out here, besides, I think your mom will agree that there are going to be some changes. Do you realize that your screwing around almost killed three people and if it wasn't for Mother, you'd have a body count?"

"It was an accident, Dad. I want to go home, can't we go home?"

"Sit down. We're staying until your mom is back to her old self."

"You can't make me. That's child abuse. I'm leaving," Justin said, his voice rising into a shriek.

"Go ahead, have a nice walk, while you're out making calls, you should call the cops, add that your carelessness almost killed three people. I'm sure that would interest them." Rory dropped down onto a chair.

Justin couldn't believe it and he stomped off to a corner seat where he could sulk in peace. He wanted to leave, but he was so hungry and tired that it would have to be another day.

Mother took her place at the head of the room's grandest table, a beast that seated forty-two residents.

"Oh fathers and mothers of moon, fire, soil, water, and sun, we thank you though you never ask for thanks. We love and need though you never needed the likes of us. This bounty is worth all our breaths for a thousand autumns. Please let us go on enjoying your world. We pray your power never drifts beyond our reach and we pray you always let us live on your backside in peace." Mother lifted her hands above her head and focussed her eyes onto the ceiling. "Continue to bless our land and air, my soul for soil."

The group repeated, and for the first time this included Rory, "My soul for soil."

~

Juliette spent the day in and out of sleep, usually waking to find Mother applying earthy balm to her chest. It was a comfort, much nicer than sitting in a loveless hospital while the busy little bees did their best to ship you off, ready or not, to mend on your own.

Outside had darkened. Her eyes fluttered at the sound of someone entering the room, it wasn't as she expected, but it was good. "Rory," she whispered.

"Oh hun, shh don't worry, it'll be all right," he said taking her hand in his.

"How bad do I look?"

"Great, beautiful, I'm so happy you're... That little bugger—" Rory cut himself off not wanting to discuss the troublesome boy.

"I know. How does it look down there?"

Rory rolled down the light blanket and stared at his wife's bare chest. Just below her breasts ran a long incision. Twine held the cut together and seemed to writhe and pulse with her heartbeats.

"I haven't looked, no mirrors."

"It's awful," Rory lifted the blanket, "but if it's going to fix you up. I'm so... you didn't... I mean, I'm happy I still have you."

Juliette squeezed his hand and attempted to smile. He gave her sips of water, explained his day, reminded her on several accounts of how much he loved her and how his life is lost without her.

Rory stepped out of Mother's house. Mother leaned by the door, puffing on a pipe.

"Mother?"

"Jeepers creepers, man!" she exclaimed holding her

pipe at her chest. "You know how old I am? I'm likely to drop ghost right on the spot. I may got to change my knickers, goodness gracious."

Embarrassed, Rory shrugged and smirked. "Juliette looks so much better, thank you. How are the others?"

"Now, you let me worry 'bout my patients," Mother said. "Ya know, sometimes I think they mix up babies, giving bad ones to good parents. Never know, I suppose maybe it's only that bad seeds can find a way into good loins. Your boy might straighten his ways someday, maybe pick a religion and be a good one, but I don't think he fits here. Not like you and your Juliette."

"Oh we don't fit that—"

"Nonsense, I never seen such a fit."

~

The moon rode low in the sky and the stars sparkled, Jody managed to turn far enough around to look out the window. She tried not to think about her head, earlier she ran her touch over a throbbing spot. The thick gauze came away as she burrowed her fingers inside, but found only another strange texture. It was coarse and almost rubbery. The fabric, if that's what it was, had a series of reinforcements built in, but she couldn't place it. She attempted to dig below the fabric, but her scalp and hair ran through.

"Fine sight isn't it?" Mother asked who'd crept into the room unnoticed.

She carried her candle and Jody fought to turn over. "Dini all right?"

"She still sleeps, but she'll wake, don't you worry 'bout her. How's the healing doing?"

Jody put her fingers to the bandage on her head.

"Now don't be messing, let the healing do as it do. Soon enough you'll be back with your girl. You're lucky to be kicking at all, lucky I got to ya in no worse for wears, if I do say so myself. At first sight, I reckoned all three of ya was goners, but nature has some power, you just gotta knows how to use it, 'course you gotta pay the debts too." Mother patted Jody's chest. "Now rest ya self."

With effort, Jody rolled back onto her side to look out the windows.

"You gonna see the stars where you going don't you worry," Mother whispered to nobody and left. She continued onto the next room, Dini's room.

The woman was indeed in much worse wear than Jody or Juliette. Cloth bandages covered her entire head, besides her eyes and mouth. Much of her chest had a cloth covering and one arm slumped useless at her side.

"Rough, but Mother going to take care, the gods take care of Mother, Mother going do the same for you."

Dini's eyes flashed open and she attempted to say something.

"Hush child, ya talking days ain't here yet, but soon, soon. The part ya get, why it might be best of all, best next to Mother I reckon. The sun and the soil all day, the moon and the soil and the rains at night, no, don't get better than that."

Mother spooned water into Dini's dry mouth. She coughed and a brown sludge forced its way from her lips. "Now don't ya fight it, you need water. All things need water to grow, ya know that, sure ya know that." She spooned more water and Dini swallowed the murk.

Mother stayed at the task for a short while and upon deciding the girl had her fill, she moved onto the next room. Juliette was in the best shape, if you ignored the bruises and keep the eyes above the chest. Mother pulled the sheet down. She ran her wrinkled fingers over the stitches that writhed and pulsed at her touch. "Coming right along and am I glad ya did, I can't do this forever," Mother whispered.

Juliette started to speak again, but Mother placed a

finger over her mouth and left the room after forcing water down the tired woman's throat. At her door, she pulled a key from her pocket and placed it into the only keyhole on the entire property. After more than ninety years, anyone is bound to have secrets. She rarely locked the door, but with visitors, one can never be too careful.

Her room was smaller than the others. There was a table with a mirror and next to that, a stool fashioned sometime in the eighteenth century. There was a squat dresser, no closet, and a tiny bed. Every year she replaced the straw inside the mattress, she patted her hand and decided a year was about up.

Mother used no pillows and had only one handmade quilt. The quilt passed generation to generation. Every time a new Mother arrived, she took care of the quilt. Yellows and browns, the quilt wasn't exactly competition worthy, but it did as it should. Mother dropped her clothing into a pile and bent to snatch the pile, she couldn't stand an untidy room. Her body sagged what little it could, most of her excess had long dried and evaporated. She placed her laundry on a side table and shuffled along the cool floor into her bed.

The quilt let out a sigh and tightened around her body. It pulsed and throbbed over her head, breathing the longevity into her lungs and heart. Within seconds, she slept and would do so until the quilt decided it was time for her to rise.

~

"Damn them all," Justin said under his breath as he paced about his small room, about ready to burst in anger. "Fuck them." He poked his head into the hallway. It was dark and silent. With his sneakers in hand, he slunk towards freedom. A familiar light snore came from his parents' room. His dad.

Justin had to talk to his mom. She'd listened to reason, surely.

It was incredibly dark. The moon and stars all hid behind light clouds that blew overhead as he watched, stopping abruptly over Naket Knoll. The rains began, as if set to timer.

He ran across the yard to Mother's house. The door creaked sounding like cannon booms to Justin's sensitive and frightened ears, but nobody came to investigate. The first room had a woman on a bed and by the shape, Justin understood that it wasn't his mother. Too boney. With light steps, Justin continued onto the next room, he looked at the body. It could've been his mother, but he wasn't certain as bandages covered her entire face. The accident ran through his mind. Nothing had struck Juliette's head. He moved out of the room, onto the next. Under foot, a series of boards creaked and Justin's heart thumped, he couldn't quite say what made him so frightened, he was, after all, just in to see his mom. But there was an atmosphere of wrongness. The third silhouette looked like his mom and his excited heart slowed. He took a long gasp for air and exhaled gently.

"Mom, Mom, wake up," he half-whispered.

Her eyes shot open and Juliette stared at her son, the father of her pain, the bad seed of her womb.

"Mom, you gotta help. This guy punched me and then they made me dig rocks all day and I didn't get a break and Dad's going crazy. Mom, we gotta get outta here. Mom?" He shook her.

"You did a terrible thing. I can hardly believe you are mine. Be good."

Justin listened in disbelief, this wasn't his mom speaking, this was that stupid old woman, it was Naket Knoll seeping into her brain, ruining her sensibility. "This is your fault, if we didn't come—"

"You're bad, be good," Juliette blasted in a loud raspy whisper.

"You're being a bitch." Justin ran from the room.

He slammed the outer door.

"Well, fuck all of you and this stupid place!" he screamed and tore off down the lane.

Nobody stopped him. He ran along the wheat and oats and the corn stalks shooting almost ready for harvest. The rain pattered over the landscape and then as if the plants and the soil explained their fill, the clouds disappeared. A small shack stood further down the lane and Justin heard a noise. An image of Horace floated into his mind and he froze in place.

Six people left the little shack, swishing and rattling as they walked. Justin managed to disengage the ice around his legs and dove into a shrub next to the lane. Two figures moved toward him and he watched. It was one woman and one man according to their shapes. The swishing and rattling grew louder. The moon floated a bright light as the clouds moved on and he saw everything he had to.

Corn stalks jutted from their collars and sleeves. They ambled more than walked while they held hands. A series of perverse scenarios played in his mind, as to why they all hid in the shack in the middle of the night. Any sexual thought died once they came within feet of him. A squeak left his lips. Their faces were *wrecked* and their eyes glowed red. They turned their focus onto his vicinity and he attempted to flee. His feet slid on the wet grass beneath him as the hands of two living scarecrows reached for him.

"You can't, nonono!"

The rough and grainy fingers scraped his skin and he shook away, his feet slipped again, and he went down. To relieve him of the terrible situation, his head struck a stone next to the path and his consciousness faded to grey.

~

Justin sat up and screamed. The sun was on the verge of showering the knoll. A few early risers gawked at him, dew and rain soaked through his clothes. He ran to the guesthouse to wake his father. There was no way they would stay if his father knew about the scarecrows.

He swung open the door and slipped again, but managed to regain his footing and tore down the hallway. He got to his father's room and found it empty.

"Ready for work?" a mannish voice asked from behind him.

He spun and looked up at the blonde haired man. "Horace." Justin began to whimper.

"Come, we're going out to the fields, we need to build stands." Horace put a firm hand on Justin's shoulder.

Justin hadn't a clue as to what building stands might mean and that didn't matter, he didn't want to do it on principal. He shook his shoulder away from Horace. "I have to change."

"Fine, change."

"I'm not stripping in front of you. You pedophile. Pervert."

"Fine," Horace said with surprising ease.

Justin changed hastily, noticing for the first time black streaks up the back of his clothing. "They dragged me back... the scarecrows," he whispered. A window sat on the far side of the room, plenty big enough to squeeze through and be done with Naket Knoll.

He swung his legs and slinked down in a limbo fashion to the grass. Excited, he ran, getting no more than two and a half steps from the house before a firm hand closed on his shoulder.

"Ready to go, I see."

"I wanna go home."

"You can go any time you want, come we'll walk together. I'd appreciate some assistance with the stands first. How about this, you help me drag out the logs and then after that you're free to go? Back to your television and air conditioning."

Justin wanted to believe his words. Part of him actually did believe and he stumbled along Horace's side.

Along the courtyard's perimeter were a series of out buildings, angled to lead toward the barn. Two buildings to the east of the barn was the wood shop and Justin followed Horace inside. Another man, Hans was his name, stood over an eight inch squared beam chipping a groove into the side. He was an older man and worked with slow methodical strokes, but none fell as he'd hoped.

"How's it coming, Dad?" Horace asked.

"Not my finest, not by a long one, might be my worst. I don't know why we don't reuse the damn things—"

"Everyone deserves their own stand, it's a tough job. It's their consolation. I…"

"I'd like that job," Hans interrupted his son.

"… don't think they'd like to sit on the old stands— What? You? Your eyes are about as strong as moldy corn husk." Horace laughed.

"I 'spose you're right, but there was a time for me, as you have now and someday, unfortunately I won't be around to gloat when you'll become a slow moving feeble old goat like me."

"Easy now. Are you done?"

Hans nodded toward a wheelbarrow brimming with beams and planks. "You'll want to carry this last guy."

Horace glanced at Justin who took the seven-foot beam. He looked at the beam wondering how in the Hell he was to carry the thing, Horace read his face. "Drag it on your shoulder. See you at supper, Dad."

"If I make it that long." Hans sat back against a wall

on a small stool.

Horace led the way out of the shed and Justin followed. The beam rode his shoulder and he felt strangely like Jesus, as if the beam represented death, a punishment for being who he was. It was heavy, hard work and Horace had to slow his pace to allow Justin to keep in stride.

They followed a path away from the courtyard. Justin passed a scarecrow that looked like a normal scarecrow, dead. Not even dead really, never living, stuffed with straw and corn stalks. Its face was so simplistic he almost laughed at his fear and imagination.

There was no doubt that he saw people, but not living scarecrows. Naket Knoll wasn't a demonic netherworld. It was just a place where people took braindead vacations.

It was a sea of fields as far as Justin could see, they'd traveled beyond the shack and took a western turn into a field of oats, doing their best to avoid trampling.

"It is a little out of season to put up new ones, but we get'm when we get'm," Horace said, lowering the wheelbarrow.

Beneath the planks and beams, sat two shovels and Horace dug them out.

"Here, don't stomp." Horace handed Justin a shovel.

Justin followed Horace once again. About sixty-feet into the field sat a small dirt mound, clear of plant life. A broken beam poked up from the soil. One and one made two in Justin's mind and he realized he and Horace were about to make new scarecrow stands. The trip wasn't about putting an end to a troublesome boy, but to put up scarecrow stands, it was obvious that his parents, no matter how they acted, didn't want him to run away. All the work was a tough love kind of thing.

Sure, that's what it is, but they had the wrong man

for the job.

Justin thought about the scarecrows and what Horace had said. "I don't get it, why wouldn't you put the scarecrows in the shed until you put seeds down, that's what they do right, scare the birds?"

"Partly," Horace said. "Dig."

Justin looked down at the dirty mouth of the shovel and then to the back of Horace's head. "No!" he shouted and slammed the shovel over the wide skull. A vibration rode the wooden shaft of the shovel and into Justin's palms.

Horace fell forward and Justin trampled his way through the field toward the forest that ran the entire edge of the Naket Knoll.

The stark difference between the field and the forest shivered through Justin. The sun blared with almost violent rays of comfort and no more than a few dozen feet into the forest, rain pounded the earth. A cool breeze floated from around the tree, inviting Justin in, and although it was dark, it rained heavy like frost slush, and it felt more like home. He'd spent his entire life in the rain. Sure, the sun came out once in a while, but for the most part home was soggy. It always rains in Vancouver.

He jogged toward the downpour, with each step his brain said he should've been closer, but his eyes told another story. A stick snapped behind him, he spun expecting to see Horace coming from the field, but there was no Horace, and there was no field. It was gone, all of it. His pace quickened and snapping sticks sounded in an eerie chorus around him. Dark fell in a visible line like an old tube TV running its last program. The trees swayed and creaked in the heavy wind. Crunching leaves and more snapping branches called his attention to something behind him, too dark to see.

"Who's there?" he whispered, wishing he hadn't

discarded his shovel.

No voice answered his call. Instead, a swishing rustling din circled him.

"I'm not afraid of you!" This was an obvious lie as his voice cracked with horror.

Glowing red eyes snapped open in a wave-like motion, clicking wetly. Justin's vision followed the eyes around the circle. Tears finally dropped down his cheeks, all hope gone.

"They said I could leave," he whimpered and sank.

"They lied," a gravelly voice said. A rough hand brushed over the boy's cheek.

He cowered away from the fingers, they couldn't be real, he knew that, but there they were, running along his skin, more and more, touching him. They tore away his shirt and then pants. He fought and screamed and squirmed. It did him no good. The leaves beneath his skin were mucky and putrid.

Those red eyes. He saw nothing but those red eyes floating in the dark sky. A heavy hand shoved Justin onto his back while fingers tugged at his arms and legs, stretching him out into a star. For a moment, he considered giving in to the demands of the demons about his body, but the snapping of elastic and tearing of the cotton of his underwear shot him into frenzy.

"No, no, don't—you can't!" He closed his eyes and struggled. He'd seen *Deliverance*. He'd watched *Oz* late nights on HBO.

His body lifted and he felt the rough and scaly fingers running up his thighs, bypassing his testicles and tickling at the crests of his ass cheeks. Then they parted.

"Nonono!"

His body fell hard, his brain went out for what seemed a blink in time. He opened his eyes and saw the barn around him. Aware of his freedom, he instinctively covered himself. Next to him, a very young looking girl began to cry, she ran from the barn, her body bare and bruised.

Justin shook his head, he couldn't explain how he'd gotten back or why he was with the girl. This was a girl he'd attempted to avoid since he'd arrived at Naket Knoll. Her name was Toffee, just like the candy, and she'd followed Justin, making gaga eyes and doing her best to flirt. It would've been flattering had she been older than eleven or twelve.

"What am I... what is she...?" he asked the stuffy dusty air of the straw mow, he couldn't piece it together. It didn't make any sense. *Why was she naked?* His hands roved to his tender underside. *Did they...?*

Below, a door slammed open and the sound of several angry men entered the barn. Toffee came back to mind. What had happened? He considered how things looked.

Things didn't look good at all.

~

Rory awoke early, long before sunrise, with an urge, a need. He washed his face and dressed. He wasn't certain where he had to be, but he knew he had to be *somewhere*. There was a general rumble coming from the kitchen behind the dining hall, he decided that *somewhere* did not abolish the need for coffee. There were a dozen or so men and women in the dining area. These were the first string of workers. Rory poured a coffee and sat at an empty table. The cooks and cleaners ignored him as he sipped. The sun was about to shed a light and his watch told him it was almost five. He decided to walk, seek out the urge of location.

Although the accident made a horrid dent in the overall scheme of his vacation, he couldn't remember ever feeling so good about his life. If Justin hadn't done what he had, they'd be all sleeping their final hours at Naket Knoll and then readying to head back down to civilization, back to stress, back to rushing, rushing, rushing. To a point, it was best that Juliette lay injured.

"Go to her," a familiar voice said.

Rory looked around and as if by some supernatural ability, Mother walked in stride with him. "Oh, gees, you scared me half to death." He put a hand to his chest.

"Ha, get what ya dish then. Juliette is awake, might be early as tomorrow that she can walk."

"I'll go see her, now's fine?"

Mother nodded. "Talk to her, tell how you feel, how the Naket Knoll feels right as rain, right as the sun, right as the soil beneath ya feet."

If it wasn't Mother speaking, if it wasn't her warm welcoming person, hearing his unexpressed thoughts spill out like a buffet menu might irk the good vibe, but Mother had a way. Rory jogged to Mother's home where his wife lied in wait.

Mother followed at a distance, fidgeting with a leather pouch dangling from her neck. She stopped by the kitchen for coffee before visiting Rory and Juliette.

It was quiet inside Mother's building, Juliette and Rory spoke in hushed breaths. Mother made sure to allow the door to bang on her way in. "Got some coffee, perk yas up a bit," she called in a warm and gentle voice.

The trio made small talk about the crops and the vacation, how great it's been outside the accident. Speaking of the accident brought around the discussion of Justin.

"Here, we raise them all, as a community. It keeps the good little ones from being bad little ones. That boy of yours, he's trouble, sorry to say." Mother was solemn. Rory and Juliette sipped their coffees in between nodding. "We mind our own, but since we didn't have no say 'bout the boy as a young'n, well, it's up to you."

"I don't want to speak out of turn, but... I wish we never had him. Hell, outside you," Rory said, placing his hand on Juliette's shoulder as he spoke, "I don't care much for anything about our old lives. I know it may sound cruel and all to talk about a kid, our kid, like that but... Oh, I don't know."

Juliette's face drew a long grave expression and then rolled scalp-bound in a half smile. "I'm so glad it isn't just me." She took a sip of coffee. "You know, I can't really remember even wanting him, since I've been in here I've forgotten so many of the pointless things."

Rory smiled and gave a slow nod, but it was only part of him. The old life had its benefits and Justin never asked for life. This fact stabbed at him like ice cream brain freeze. They'd forced life on him. Juliette had wanted a baby. He'd wanted a baby. Justin never had an option.

"That's very nice to say and ya both welcome to stay, but ya gotta do something 'bout that rascal. He was out screwing around with the scarecrows last night."

They listened, yawning.

"If it was up to me, I'd run the court on him," Mother said, leading the parents to a conclusion she wanted them to reach.

With a gentle nudge, Rory convinced Juliette to share her bed, he slipped off his shoes and lied back, listening, no longer grasping. Juliette sipped at her cup, but couldn't finish and set it aside.

"Don't ya want your coffee?" Mother asked.

"I'm still not one-hundred percent just yet," she said. "Look at this one though, sleeping like a baby. Maybe I ought to give him the whole bed, perhaps I can take a short—"

"No!" Mother said and then recovered her volume. "I reckon ya gonna bust ya stitches if ya rush things, besides, ya really ought to rest, keep them fluids up too.

Ya body's goin' through quite a juggle in there, out with the old bad and in with the new good."

Juliette pursed her dry lips, looking longingly at the sun shining through the cloudy glass over the window.

"Drink the coffee." Mother stared down, stern as a librarian two days from retirement.

Juliette followed orders and drowsiness lifted like a coroner's blanket.

Mother went to check on the other patients. The change was almost through and Jody looked as Mother hoped: her flesh hardened in a pale brown tone, blackness coursing through her veins and arteries, bulging just beneath her new skin. Her fingers were dehydrated-kernel-ridden sticks, her arms strong stocks, her legs even stronger stocks, and her hair a crazy mop of golden brown threads.

Jody blinked her eyes open, revealing two fires that burned, light or dark, in her sockets, cutting through the air. She licked her grainy lips with a papery tongue riddled with minute oat buds. "Dini," she managed.

"Hush, hush, no need for fussing. I'm 'bout to check on her, but *you*, thank the gods above and below, ya turning out right, just right, I reckon. Ya gonna be happy from here on. I'm a little envious of ya, not that there's anything wrong with envy. Oh ya gonna spend a lifetime with the gods." Mother petted the dried husk flesh of Jody's shoulder.

"What… happened… to…?" Jody closed her eyes and lost the sentence to time.

"Ya not gonna worry much 'bout speaking like people, darling. A fine one, ya gonna be a fine one."

Mother moved onto the next room.

The easy happiness she found with Jody evaporated when she stepped into Dini's room. "Poor thing." She looked onto the moulding corpse bespattered with hungry flies. "Murderer now, I 'spose. That boy doing me a favor by killing ya. In a way, ya did the gods, did the Knoll, did Mother a great favor."

After initiating a cleanup of the decomposing woman, Mother turned her attention back onto Rory, his mind was right, but his body wasn't. Juliette took in air from cornstalk lungs, transplanted in order to preserve her life. Rory needed a piece of his own to belong to Naket Knoll. It can get in the mind without a cut, but it takes the knife to put the Knoll in to the blood.

A heart is at its strongest when it's of the soil and the sky. Mother readied a small team and made the first incision into his chest.

~

It was a setup, the whole thing, and unnecessary since Dini passed, but wheels in motion take effort to stop and why bother? Mother needed a boy so guilty no parental love or need remained. The rape of a girl might do it or the manslaughter of a woman in the wrong place at the wrong time might do it, but both together left no question.

Justin had put on his clothing, leaving his legs half in and half out by the time the vigilante squad found him. They took him with firm hands and, to his surprise, without harming him. He pleaded, "I didn't touch her!"

But the arguments had no effect. They dragged him, limpness his only defense, behind the barn, the pens, and the stable. Beyond it all, sat a tiny shack with heavy log walls running north south and east west. It was a cage, one difficult to peer into, though undoubtedly a prison.

One man held Justin while two men and a burly woman spun a lever and pulley system. At one end sat an enormous stone and at the other a heavy wooden door. They grunted and groaned but the lever turned the wheel far enough to toss Justin inside the shack cage.

He stumbled across the small room and fell into a dusty pile of straw. There, it seemed as if eternity began to set in. Hour after hour passed and nothing happened, nobody came, Justin watched the pigs, the cows, and the horses, or did his best to. The grass around the cell was going on five-feet, meaning the animals had to be standing upright and in the case of the pigs, standing on a hill.

"Poison," he said to himself. "When Mom gets up—"

The supper bell jangled and a little later Roderick approached the cell, plate and jug in hand. He didn't say a word and handed the food through the slots.

"Hey, I wanna talk to my mom," Justin whimpered.

Roderick shrugged and headed back through the livestock yard. Dry oatmeal and a cold cob of corn, it was what constituted of his prison meal. The jug held what appeared to be water, Justin wondered how many had spit in it, perhaps even pissed in it. He set it aside. He was hungry enough to ignore the possibilities of special food preparation. He tackled the corn first and then ate the ground oats. He then had to submit to his thirst and drank water in order to get the dry goods down. The sun lingered, but eventually fell.

Night was a bad time.

Fearful of the floating red eyes, Justin buried himself in the straw and managed a few hours' sleep before the rooster called on the sun to rise. He blinked and a sharp blade of straw scratched at his pupil, bringing around immediate consciousness and pain.

"Hello!" And when he got no answer, he repeated his call. The cattle joined his song and fussed in chorus. It was still dim, but neither sun nor moon claimed the sky. The horses didn't move, the pigs didn't come into view, both remained silent, but the cows played and yelled, helping Justin's task. A loud whistle ran through the yard and the cows quieted.

"Who's there?" Justin said, hearing footsteps approaching.

The grass blocked the view of the path beyond a few feet, but Justin saw the eyes, they burned into the air like the tails of sparklers. He backed to the wall furthest from the door and watched them. Thinking about the lever and pulley gave him a sense of safety, it took three people to open the door and there was but one *person* at his cell now.

The scarecrow turned the lever with ease and the rock rose into the air. The not person entered and Justin sank in fear, tears rolling down his face. He closed his eyes and listened to the thing inch closer. Hands latched onto him and pulled him downward. The hands became gentle and Justin became a statue. His zipper zipped its familiar voice, downward.

"No, please, please don't."

Cotton shifted over his hips. Past his thighs. Drifting beyond his ankles. Before long, he was once again bare naked as the night.

"God, no, don't."

The scarecrow laughed and Justin opened his eyes, it was daylight and he sat in his cell, penis in his palm. The entirety of Naket Knoll, excluding the visiting vacationers, looked in on him with a mixture of disgust and humor. Justin spilled sideways to cover his shame.

"Devil bum if I ever seen one," a woman said from behind his back.

Mother's familiar voice agreed and suggested that soon enough his parents would pass the judgment. Justin dressed, again, and felt a little better hearing that his fate was up to his parents. He spent much of the day thinking about the scarecrows who, so far, hadn't done anything but give him a couple good scares.

Through the day, Justin received two meals and two jugs of water. He urinated through the cell into the long grass and hoped his parents would get him out of the place before he had to take a number two.

The moon filled the sky and Justin again buried his body in the straw. In the morning, he didn't call out and nobody came, neither human nor demon. Waiting in silence was a hard lesson and he thought about how much he missed home, wondering how long he'd have to stay in Naket Knoll.

"Why'd they make me come to this stupid place?" he said, as he sat in a corner, his arms crossed over his knees. "'Cause you're bad and get into shit."

Mid-morning Jacob replaced the quiet Roderick as sustenance distributor. Justin cowered at the sight of something different. Jacob slid a plate of corn meal and cold mashed potatoes into the cell.

Justin didn't make a move. "Hey, I need your jug... trade ya," Jacob said. "Move it."

Stretching out without leaving a backside pivot, Justin pushed the wooden jug to the edge of the cell. Jacob grabbed his foot and smiled, his teeth yellowed with hints of brown. The fingers dug, nails cresting blood moons in his flesh. Justin kicked free.

"One of those womens died you know? I seen't her body. You gonna pay for that, you're a little murderer and a raper and you hit Horace with a shovel. He ain't happy 'bout that one." Enjoyment spread across Jacob's crusty lips.

"No I didn't... In the barn was 'cause the thing was too old. Why was it there?"

"Don't matter, don't matter at all, not how we do things here. It's up to yer Ma and Pop, if you was one of us, we would'a already fed you to the scarecrows. Have you met the scarecrows, little murderer?" Justin's head rose and his cheeks drained of color. "Guess ya have, they nice, most of'm are womens, ya know? Some of'm is mens, but most is womens. That's a bad way to go, they don't just eat ya and get it over with, naw, they play with ya, like a pussy plays with a mouse. Actually, maybe more like a mutt plays with a shoe."

~

Jody held her eyes tight. Mother's voice was close by, speaking to a man and a woman in another room. She heard an explanation of Dini's death and the retribution for the boy, he needed to pay, *that's the natural way*, Mother had said. But that wasn't right. It was an accident, it was horrible that Dini died and maybe it was only that Jody really wanted to cool it with Dini that she took such a soft stance on the boy, but the world didn't need any more frost to the constant winter of the universal heart.

She sat up and looked at her arms. She had to stifle a cry of alarm. Her skin had all melted away in favor of cornhusk and wheat stems. The tongue in her mouth rolled about with harsh edges, it wasn't right either. She shook. "No, no, no, can't be." The air caught in her throat and the bristled rustle in her chest made her shudder.

Mother had turned her into a monster.

What did she do to me? Dini died for this mess? You'd be alive if you didn't always have to fix things... Goddamn you, Dini, if you'd just admitted it was over. Jody's thoughts fell quiet and she dropped back onto her bed when she heard the sound of approaching steps, doing her best to play a sleeping bag of leaves.

Mother stepped in the room. "Jody, wake up. You're good as new, look better than new if ya ask me, uh-hmm." Mother loomed over the frightened former woman.

An unavoidable and involuntary shiver ran through Jody's body, rustling her dry stalks. She waited, the jig was up, but Mother didn't make a sound.

Jody opened her eyes to an empty room. A heavy breath expelled from whatever she had inside that worked as her lungs. It was almost black, but she saw as clearly as if it was day, a sunny day. She rocked her corn stalk and tree limb legs over the edge of her tiny bed. Her feet swished and scraped against the floor. She took as few steps as possible, horrified, as if at any moment Mother might appear and perform a new pagan science experiment on her body.

It wasn't until the cool night air and the pelting rain hit her body that she realized her nakedness. She looked down, it was shameful, but for all the wrong reasons. She wished for her sagging breasts. They'd embarrassed her before, but that was then, that was gravity, nothing as awful as the oat patches resting in little mounds, sure they're high again, but... She took her hard and rigid little fingers and ran them toward where her sex used to reside. It was still there, but not the same, nothing was. Everything about her body held tough edges, as if her skin grew a series of crooks like coffee table corners to smack knees and dent baby foreheads.

A scream built in her chest. She let it go, it sounded like a whistle, wind whipping through the railing of a ferry during a rough day at sea. It stung her ears and garnered attention from others.

Little red eyes bobbed through the air from every corner of the courtyard. Even from hundreds of feet, Jody saw heads nod and organic smiles stretch. It made her stomach gurgle and bubble, a downward rush pressed into her bowels. She couldn't move. Waited. The eyes ceased watching her. She wanted to leave, but didn't know how. The rest of the world would take an eager eye to her condition, but how could they help? Gawkers, civilization is a world of inactive gawkers. Everybody loves to see horror, to bask and roll like shit-filthy pigs.

A sudden urge to keep this secret blazed within. She wouldn't be a freak, never. "Suicide. Kill yourself," she said in a whisper that sounded as if speaking while someone crunched dry leaves. She then recalled Mother's proximity and ran.

Avoiding the eyes dictated direction. They were suddenly everywhere, those glowing promises of terror. She wanted a peaceful place to think and steady her monstrous hands. A place to end it all.

In the distance, beyond the barnyard, a river rushed, offering her an answer. She ran toward the sound of animals.

~

Justin couldn't sleep. There were scratchy steps approaching. They swished with scarecrow feet. He sobbed. He imagined those creepy eyes and those rough fingers running along his body.

He shook, much of the straw fell from his back. Uncovered and terrified, he couldn't help himself as the steps drew closer and closer.

~

Jody attempted a run, but her legs wobbled and her chest heaved. This new body was suited to a sedentary life. She heard sobbing. It was not animalistic, but it was interesting. The corn of her brain muddying somewhat, shifting her view. She spotted the noise. It was the boy, the poor boy that had to join his parents on a pioneer retreat. The cell's door sat closed and she understood a little more about what Mother meant. The woman expected retribution and until then, unlawfully imprisoned a boy who was bored of the boring existence that Naket Knoll celebrated.

Veering from the path and toward the cell, Jody attempted to call out to the boy, but only a low whistle left her lips accompanied by a rustling mumble. She opened the cell's door. The sobs increased, the boy's body shook and rattled, half buried in dirty straw. He stank of piss and shit. Jody fought her nose—or whatever worked that sense since her transformation—

and approached the boy. As soon as her long twiggish fingers grazed his arm, he spun with wild eyes and a high-pitched squeak.

The intention was to free the boy, but something shifted further. The corn of her mind finding grains and stamping out human impulse. Her face contorted into an enormous grin, a laugh escaped her throat, and she pawed at his skin leaving harmless white lines of terror on the outside of his epidermis. The more he squealed and squirmed, the more pleasure she took from the incident.

It was nothing short of satiating, a craving met, an urge, a need, all of it beautiful—to scare, to scare was to live! Jody screamed in pleasure, she read the boy's fears as if presented on a movie reel before her eyes.

She drank of his terror, the one furthered by the first scarecrows tasted sweetest, those fears of rape. *Strange fear for a small boy,* she thought and opened his jeans. An image played and Jody understood more and more. It wasn't just a fear built by the scarecrows. The boy watched too much TV, too many nasty films for his age. It fueled her need, she ran her hands along his sides and flipped him onto his face, his soiled underpants came down and she grazed his cheeks with her sharp fingers. A tip scratched at the hidden pucker.

It was not her duty to do more.

Frantic, she tore out of the barnyard, through the courtyard and down the lane. She saw the shack, she saw the others, she saw her family and they saw her. Crunchy, swishy arms wrapped around her body and she was home.

Justin's cell door remained open.

~

It wasn't as it was the other times when the scarecrows came, he didn't open his eyes to a terrible reality, he was in his cell, naked again, or mostly, but this time he was alone. Hastily, he crawled towards freedom, jeans in hand, and ran to the barn, sticking to the shadows. It was a dark night thanks to the rainclouds overhead and when he crossed into the courtyard, he didn't see anyone, not even a set of the evil red eyes. Light from the forever-lit dining hall cast little shadows over the world, revealing the sleeping figures within some of the homes.

The plan was to find his parents, explain what they'd done to him and get away from that place. A sickly feeling bounced into his stomach as he turned the handle to Mother's house, that was the last place he saw his mom and was certain he'd find a welcoming ear once he found her.

The floor creaked under his foot, but he continued, the hell-with-it approach. "Mom," he called in a voice a little louder than conversational.

Juliette sat up on the bed and lifted an index finger to her mouth. She was dressed and looked fine, but Rory slept shirtless and almost glowed against the darkness of the room. Justin didn't know how to react, his mom obviously wasn't happy to see him.

"Mom!"

Rory sat up, the blanket fell from his bare chest. A long pinkish scar ran up from below his left breast.

"Ugh, can't you do anything you're told? Can't you see that your father was resting? How did you get out anyway?"

Justin considered a response to every question as he heard them but the third and final left him dumbfounded. "You knew?"

"Knew what?" Rory asked.

"That they had me in a cell?" Justin asked.

"Well of course we knew, we were going to pass judgment tomorrow. I don't know what your hurry is. You know one of those women died. Mother said it was up to us to decide your punishment. I think I'd like to hand the duty away, let the Naket Knoll justice system decide, they're pretty smart around here," Juliette said and then laid back as if the explanation settled everything.

"Go back to your cage, would ya?" Rory said.

"Are you fucked?" Justin yelled, both Rory and Juliette sat up. "This place has demons, I saw them. Living scarecrows. If you leave me in that cell they'll kill me. They're all fucked, they pray to the moon and the sun—"

Rory said, "You're fucked."

"You broke the main rule," Juliette added. Justin saw the gentle line of her mouth thanks to her brushing and whitening regiment.

Outside, the home doors started to creak open and slam shut.

"You're my parents, you can't let them lock me away. I didn't even get a trial, come on Dad, you know that isn't right," Justin begged, using what hoped were the keywords to his father's understanding.

Light flooded the room and two men took Justin's arms. He didn't fight back, he couldn't, the light shed the true image of Rory. His skin had greened, his body appeared a day from emaciated, and the stitches on his chest held puffy and infected flesh together.

"Look what they've done to you," Justin whispered.

"You did this to me," Juliette said in a *you're getting as you deserve tone*.

"Not you, Dad. Look at him, Mom!" Justin shouted as the two men pulled him away.

"Oh," she said. She'd grown accustomed to everyone worrying over her, she hadn't really thought of anyone but Mother in days. Juliette's eyes took a long look at Rory, finally noticing his color, noticing the way his body carried extra skin as if something worked on erasing him from the inside, and noticing that whatever Mother saw fit to do wouldn't take. "That's not good." She was visibly disappointed.

"No, but Mother will fix it," Rory said. "I need some rest, best go back to your cage until tomorrow." He dropped back onto his pillow.

The boy shouted and kicked to no avail the entire journey.

The cell door clanked shut and the men left. Justin sat on the deflated pile of straw and looked out into the grass. He found two sets of red eyes glaring back at him. He wondered if it was like what people say when you go camping, see one set of racoon eyes and don't see another dozen out there. He hoped not, but they decided to leave him alone for the night, for whatever reason.

Eventually, Justin drifted off to sleep, dreaming of scarecrows. Real scarecrows that acted mostly as bird perches in fields.

They really didn't do anything.

He awoke to the sound of the rooster. The sun was ready to master the sky, clouds formed from out of nowhere and owned the sky. It was dark once again. The scarecrows with their deep red eyes approached the cell. Having pretty well given up on life, Justin watched, he didn't cower, he didn't sob, he sat and watched.

Somewhere deep down, a notion from a dream swirled in his subconscious.

The cell door opened and the scarecrows ushered Justin out. He walked as if approaching the gallows. He put his head down, trying to think of a way to freedom. The group stopped and Justin bumped into the scarecrow in front of him. It didn't offend and Justin took a step backwards and gazed around the courtyard. A series of great flaming torches circled him. The residents stood the perimeter and watched. Mother, Rory, and Juliette were inside the ring of fire with him.

The scarecrows backed away to the edges, the residents, the people, stepped further from the demons, feigning a need for a better view to mask their fears.

Justin looked at his parents. Rory leaned on Juliette's arm and glared in slack-jawed amazement over the ominous presence of something otherworldly happening. Juliette looked forward to Mother, smiling as if in love.

"We, the children of the soil, the fire, the water, the sun, of all the gods of below and above, we folks, ask ya to pass judgment down on the troublesome boy," Mother spoke as if attempting to recall something written, working hard to forfeit her typical lingo as she did with the supper prayer. "Parents of the boy, ya word stands, how does ya choose?"

Juliette's smile widened and she looked toward Rory. They'd discussed the answer. She knew his heart was like her heart, in a sense. Juliette began the planned speech, "We want to hand the response—"

Rory saw it differently while they'd walked. His heart was sick. The magic of the place was no longer like a wonderful drug, but rather, a poison streaming through his veins. "He's leaving now," Rory said. "I think I need a hospital."

"Rory?"

"This place is stealing something from in here," he tapped on his temple, "and in here," he touched his fingers on his chest, running the tips along the inflamed flesh. "They're trying to steal our lives, our time." He spoke feeling that his life came down to that moment. He wanted to say something meaningful, poetic, but that was the best he could manage. "We aren't the same people that came here, they've changed us, she's changed us. I'm not right."

Mother looked at Juliette with a concerned brow, but what she heard brought about a smirk. "Well, I'm not going anywhere," Juliette said turning back to Mother and lifting her nose, above it all.

"Juliette, look at me, look at me... please." Juliette turned to her husband. "I'm dying and whatever that woman did to me is killing me."

"Killing is in the eye of the grains. Ain't none of us gonna stop ya though, can't speak for them." She sneered and pointed toward the scarecrows.

"It's too late for me to worry about anybody in a suit," Rory said as he shifted from Juliette to Justin.

"Be judgment passed, my soul for soil," Mother said.

The residents, including Juliette, echoed the phrase. Justin helped his father limp out of the ring. They walked past Horace. He had a bruise down his neck and fire in his eyes, upset about never paying out the retribution deserved.

They continued toward the gravel road that met the lane to Naket Knoll. The dark cloud cover followed their movements. Occasionally, a scarecrow tried his hand, but neither Justin nor Rory offered any fear to feast. Justin understood something and Rory had no clue.

They reached the road after some time, Rory collapsed. Justin helped his father sit up, then rise. The scarecrows waited, watched, powerless, and let them pass.

Three hours of slow trudging, Justin waved down a transport truck, a massive Peterbilt with polished chrome everywhere. The driver had only the seat next to him to carry a passenger, no place for an ailing man and his son. He radioed for an ambulance and then continued on.

Rain fell in fat drops. By the time the ambulance arrived, Rory's clothing stuck to his skin, showing his ribs and collarbone, it appeared only cotton separating insides from atmosphere.

"They did something to him," Justin said, his voice heated and excited. "His chest, his chest."

"Yeah, I see it. Calm down," the paramedic said in a soft tone as she unbuttoned Rory's shirt and upon seeing the work. The writhing and pulsing threads and the puffy red and green skin were too much. "Our Father who…" she trailed off and fingered at a small crucifix she wore around her neck.

"No more gods, please," Justin said.

~

It didn't take long once in the hospital to discover that whatever strange fight raged within Rory's body was above the means of a small town hospital. An hour after arrival, the man who all thought would die, managed to cling to life.

Justin tried to look at the good side, soon he'd tell the cops what happened, they'd go into Naket Knoll and charge all those earth-fuckers. He also got to ride in a helicopter and that was something. The bright side was a short adventure.

Some time passed in the waiting room at St. Paul's in Vancouver and a doctor approached Justin. "Uh, Mr. Thafferthus?" He was an older man with pale fuzz for hair, a sharp contrast against his dark skin. He sat down

"Justin," he muttered, expecting bad news.

"Was your father part of a cult, or maybe did he have any crazy ideas about, oh Hell, do you know if your father had heart trouble, anything that may make him seek a naturopathic solution?" the doctor asked shifting on his feet in discomfort.

"What did they do? They were crazy." Justin looked to his hands as he tugged at threads from the old t-shirt one of the paramedics had lent him.

"Crazy, but genius. It's impossible that it worked as long as it had—impossible."

"What?"

"Someone replaced his heart with a hollowed corncob that… somehow worked with his body until his body rejected it… It was really something and if you'll allow it, I'd like to take the heart. It is quite a thing. I've never even heard of a naturopathic attempting something like that. The first naturopath I'd guess could qualify as a real doctor, not just mumbo jumbo stuff about the power of twigs and roots, I mean a—"

"So he's dead?" Justin asked.

"Oh, uh yes, he passed."

Justin stood and approached a police officer who'd returned from a smoke break.

The doctor followed. "So, can I keep the corn heart?"

Justin didn't hear him.

~

The officer listened with interest. The doctor decided once again to attempt to acquire the rights to the heart, which got the attention of the officer, solidifying the boy's statement. The heart remained in evidence, frozen and stored at the hospital of course.

Later that day, a team including helicopters and more than one-hundred officers scoured the area Justin sent them to. They found the lane, but couldn't cross as a storm wall blocked them and any airborne search.

Day after day, the police came away without answers. Eventually they took to the forest. A fire broke loose and engulfed nine officers and much of the effort. After that, the search fizzled and Justin moved in with his uncle's family. The general consensus concluded that Justin should forget and move on, much of it was obviously part of his imagination.

Months after burying his father, Justin weighed his options for college. The letter from Holland College in Charlottetown, P.E.I. offered him a spot in a computer design course. It was about as far as he could get from Naket Knoll without leaving the country.

It was okay. He got on spending the days tapping away at his computer. Before long, he'd met a girl taking a course in tourism. They dated for a while. It was the first really good thing to happen to him since the death of his father.

It was a Monday, it rained, something he'd had much experience with, and Mia ran into his dorm room, excited. She had an envelope in her hand.

"Whoa, whoa, settle yourself."

"I can't believe it, I got it 'cause I did that thing for the wildlife conservation group, that's what the letter says, that's why I got it!" Mia exclaimed, jumping like a kid getting word she'd be going to Disneyland.

"Got what?" Justin asked jumping along with her, half-mocking, half-excited.

"In exchange for doing a pamphlet for them, they offered me an all-expenses paid trip and everything, like it's amazing. I asked my prof and she says I can use it for credit, too," Mia said, settling to speak.

"Who did?" Justin thought he might just get to tag along somewhere fun.

Mia handed over an envelope. "This place." Justin held the letter and pulled the postcards from the envelope. Mia ran her finger along the handwritten letter. "Uh, Naket Knoll." Justin began shaking. "Isn't it cooky? The lady in charge calls herself Mother, that's how she signed it, look."

Justin glared at the postcard, obviously created by an outside source, as they didn't do it in the Knoll. The title ran in bright orange bubble letters: *Mother and Mother-in-Making Welcome You.* He screamed and dropped the postcard.

Mia picked it up. "What? What is it?"

Justin couldn't answer. The photo of that woman with her arm around the woman who used to be his mom standing next to a scarecrow rocked him. He stepped back to a wall and gazed with vacant fear.

"That scarecrow is amazing," Mia said. "It looks so

real. The letter says that I can bring a guest. I hope you'll come. It would be so nice to get away from it all. Really kick it, like, old school."

We, in the Dark, Together, Forever

Dust clung in the deep ridges of the old man's leathery face. The shovel in his hands sank into the rich black soil. Story was, there was oil somewhere on the farm and that kept the earth dark and loamy. Arnold Young had no interest in oil.

For years, he'd dug. The world considered him an old coot. Good with his kids and grandkids, but a coot all the same. Just as well.

Mapped, he'd sectioned his land into documented quadrants. Using the plow where possible, the loader bucket elsewhere, but most of the digging happened with a wooden-handled, clover-shaped, steel-mouthed shovel. Exhausted, head lolling on a cracking pinion, the old man leaned on the soft mud bank, trying to catch his breath in the damp summer air. For decades he'd sought, and time seemed ready to run out on him.

It was the final square in the final quadrant of forest when it hit home, in a sense. Filthy and naked, in view of a shy but interested whitetail deer, Arnold kicked the mouth of his shovel into the soil with his ragged steel-toed boot. A long white beard hung down his face. His frame was of bones and tissue paper, stained by patches of ugly liver spots and the scars of a harried existence.

A mouthful of dirt landed in the discard mound and then another and another. The hole vented partway under a tall maple tree. There, in that three-foot-deep hole, he began to cry. The last spot was as empty as the first.

Ruined and spent, he remained in the hole.

"Damn you! You movin'?"

This was a silly and impossible thought. The sky above cracked in reply. Rain pattered in heavy drops, and still, Arnold stood in that hole, leaning, crying, broken.

The promise of treasure was so real, many nights he could almost touch it, other nights he dreamed of touching it. Scanning the map of his mind, he traversed the sum of his land, quadrant by quadrant. There was nowhere he'd overlooked. Unless…

Nine hours after the rain started, it stopped. It was so obvious, so impossibly close to him for so many years. The knowledge pulled him from his broken reverie. He had to dig, but far, far from where he stood.

Renewed, Arnold tried to climb out of his hole. It wasn't much of a hole anymore. The mud rode waves and covered him to his middle.

"Ain't stoppin' me now," he mumbled. "No way."

Digging, the earth beneath him resettled and he sank by inches. Frantic, he clawed at the mud, quicker than he sank by a half.

Cleared to his knees, Arnold kicked and grabbed onto strong roots reaching from the tree trunk.

"I'm comin'. I know where it is!"

The whitetail deer was no longer shy. It bounded

toward the old man before skidding to a stop. It turned and pointed a raised tail and its gold rear. Arnold paused to stare up at the skinny beast's puckered pink asshole. Clumps of dirt rode the man's bottom half like Dalmatian spots. On hand and knee, he pushed upwards, no time to worry about this curious critter.

The whitetail leaned on its forelegs and kicked out its hind legs. The stony hooves struck Arnold's forehead. There was a crack followed closely by the sound of a flopping, lifeless body.

~

"Oh, Dad," Angela Elfman said, looking to the ceiling, thinking of the farm.

"It might feel weird, but we've been talking about change," Frank Elfman said.

They'd lived in tight quarters when Becky came along. Three people in a small duplex still meant there'd be room for everyone, but adding the fourth made things iffy and it only got worse as the kids grew.

"I never should've—" Angela started.

"Zip it," Frank said. Every time they discussed finances, he nipped her worries before she fully voiced them. "Ever hear a deathbed fogey talking about how they wished they'd put more money on the mortgage? No. They talk about missed dreams."

Angela sighed. "But maybe I should grow—"

"Bullshit. You're grown as it gets. Who knows, maybe you'll find the inspiration of *singularity* you always talk about," Frank said. Angela was a painter, a fantastic imitator, perfect lines and dimensions, but no solid voice of her own. "Becky might get pissy about the move, but I know Jeremy'll love it. He's run out of places to mine in the backyard."

A shiver ran over the bumps of her brain meat. Her father had dug as a way to deal with death and then died doing just that. Digging and dealing. The connection between her father and son was terrifying. Hopefully, Jeremy's digging was only a phase.

"What about your job?"

"Pfft, I can get a new job. There's no deep need or desire in here." Frank tapped his temple. "You've got enough for both of us. Besides, I plan on retiring after you paint your first set of masterpieces."

For the last eleven years, he'd worked at a department superstore putting together merchandise and managing the toys, seasonal, and hardware sections.

Angela had lost her job of eight years at a car battery factory seven years earlier, right after her maternity leave ended. Seventy-one job applications left her email without success, so they'd learned to live on his wage.

Doing with less was hardest on Becky and if she dealt by donning dark duds and lip liner, then so be it.

~

"Ugh, look at this place," Becky said, inside she was leaping with joy. It was so good to get away from the rich girls and maybe turn her back on this goth thing.

"I love Grandpa's!" Jeremy nearly shook out of his shoes in excitement. He wore a plastic hardhat and carried a small steel shovel from Home Depot. His father had received an employee discount on in-stock items, before he quit and helped Angela pack up the family, that is.

According to the internet searches, it was best that he didn't expect much from farming. It was the land that had value, not so much the food that came off it. They could rent the field out and still work elsewhere. It was apt to ease life by a notch or two.

~

In bed, staring at a new, but familiar ceiling, Angela explained her father's tendency toward the oblivious. After her mother died, the place fell further and further into disarray until someone said something. Arnold didn't look at the farmstead the same way the neighbors and the children had. The farmstead was a source of income and a place to dig holes in his spare time.

"What was he digging for, really?" Frank asked.

"Oh, I don't know. He said he had a dream, my mother told him to move on, we almost did, and then a few days later he decided we had to stay. He had another dream. My mother told him to find the prize."

"Grief is a devil. What was the prize?"

"He never said exactly. His prize, the treasure, whatever it was I think he thought finding *it* might bring him closer to Mom."

"Did you go digging with him?"

"Sometimes, but I always got bored. He dug without talking, always thinking of his map, staring at the dirt and mud, pick-axing stone, focussing on the never ending search."

Frank draped an arm over her chest. "I know it bugs you with the boy, but Jeremy thinks he's one of the *Seven Dwarves* or something."

"I know. It's just so damned odd. Like digging's in the blood."

Frank rolled back over, laughing. "Maybe they can test for it, like a genetic thing. Isolate it and prescribe some prenatal pills."

"Ha-ha, jerk." Angela tugged on the gold chain dangling below the old lamp next to the bed.

"Lights out!" Frank shouted upon seeing the glow down the hall.

"Going pee!" Jeremy shouted back.

"Shut up!" Becky said.

"We're like the Waltons," Angela said.

The stream of urine hitting water, followed by a flushed toilet were loud in the quiet home.

"Seat down," Frank called out after a short series of sticky sounding footfalls moved along the hall.

The seat clunked and then the feet prattled away again.

"Light off," Frank added.

"Shut up!" Becky cried out once more.

~

Jeremy took a deep breath and ran back to the washroom. The old house was spooky and he hadn't yet mastered the layout, but he was old enough that he didn't need a nightlight. Still, he should've thought about the shadowy patch in the hallway before he let his door creak nearly closed. Even with the washroom light lit, the shadow was long and scary.

"Only a shadow," he whispered and hit the switch, frozen. He flicked it back on to make sure nothing arose in the second the shadows had to fester evils. All clear.

Crouched as if to start an endurance race, his left hand reached for the light. Off he shot, taking a few steps before stopping. False start, the bulb remained aglow. He settled toes on the imaginary starting line, hand on the switch, eyes forward. Click. Off. His feet smacked against the aged hardwood and his palm banged on his door at the end of the hallway. Light showered over him and he huffed at the *wimpy hallway shadows*.

He didn't have a lamp next to his bed and didn't think of it until that second. The Tazmanian Devil on his alarm clock howled soundlessly, offering him some protection. Still... He readied for another race, his hand on the light switch, eyes on the soft finish line only five steps across the room. Click. Off. He launched after four steps, and landed on his bed, rolling under the soft fortress-like walls of his blanket. The darkness had him surrounded.

~

"I don't believe my eyes," Arnold Young said.

It was dark, but Jeremy was fairly certain he wasn't

in his new bedroom anymore. First off, he didn't feel the bed beneath him. Second, his grandfather was in the ground.

"That's you, ain't it?" Arnold carried a candle and his voice seemed to come from everywhere.

The flame approached slowly.

"Grandpa, you're dead," the boy said, echo fading into the vast blackness surrounding him.

"You're dreamin'. I'm visitin' my grandboy in a dream, no harm, no foul."

Jeremy understood that dreams were the things his brain created to eat time while he slept. "Okay."

The candle drew close enough that Jeremy saw his grandfather's tired face smiling beneath a long white beard. Jeremy thought it must be how he looked before he died, because he never saw him with a beard like that.

Seeing him, the question arose. He'd heard his parents discussing the topic much since his grandfather died. "Were you digging for gold? I wanna find gold so I can take everybody on a surprise trip to Disneyworld."

"I can show you a better place than Disneyworld." Arnold touched a cold hand on Jeremy's shoulder.

"But just a dream place. I dream places all the time," Jeremy said, an expert on the topic. "Dream places don't mean nothing."

"You couldn't be more wrong, boy. That's what I was diggin' for, bring it together, the good dream place with the real awake place."

"You can't do that. Doesn't work, dreams are like movies in my head. Dad told me."

"Sure they are, but they got to shoot movies, don't they? And they shoot the movies in real places, better places. You mix the two places and woo-wee!"

"Oh."

"You got to find the right spot to dig and I can tell you where. I looked over the whole darn place before I figured it out. Was right under my nose."

"You know where there's treasure?" Jeremy whispered, conspiracy underway.

"Sure do. You can use my diggin' tools, too. I left them out by the maple tree in the north field." Arnold blew out the candle.

Jeremy opened his eyes and yawned. It was morning and he had some tools to find.

~

Fetching groceries, Frank and Angela left the kids at home. Angela had settled into work around the house. Originality forever scratching on the outskirts of thought while she strolled the aisles. At the front of the store, Frank borrowed a pushpin from the notice of a library day camp cancellation already a week into the past.

"That the land at the Young farm?" a voice asked from behind him.

Frank turned to look at a large man with a soft middle, and big, hard-looking arms. Natural layered muscle all over, bulky, though not hulking like a body builder.

"Uh, yeah," Frank said.

The man wore a scowl. "You can take that sign down. 'Less you asking a stupid amount."

"I… You want to rent it?" Frank caught on and the scowl twisted into a grin.

"I live next door. I'm Mike Gum and this is my— hey, get over here."

A boy stepped from behind a cardboard ballot sign for Lay's potato chips. *Win a trip to Pittsburgh, spend a day with the Penguins*. The son was tall and gangly. There were a few red mounds on his neck, acne mixed with a patchy beard.

"This is Scott."

Scott held out a hand.

Frank shook two hands, stated his name once.

By the time Angela finished gathering the basics and a few extras, she found her husband at the front of the store, all smiles with the flyers in hand.

"I thought you were gonna put them up?"

Frank explained meeting the neighbors.

"Said he'd be by after supper with a check. It's a real load off. I didn't want to worry you, but what if it's a month or two before I find another job?"

"I know, I know," Angela said.

At home, Becky helped with the groceries. She'd dressed *normally*, her gothic choices set aside while there was nobody around to impress. Angela hoped that Becky had her eyes on a future dressing like a *normal girl*.

"Where's your brother?" Frank asked.

Becky shrugged and picked up two bags by their cotton handles. "He said he was going to look for digging stuff. I saw him out by the little shed like an hour ago."

"Remember, he's still young. You've got to watch him some," Frank said.

"I didn't make him," she said, and that was true, but it was no good.

Becky headed straight to the small shed after dropping off the groceries. She called out twice. A hook and eye latched the shed door. The area was mostly grass and gravel. The under-used outbuildings had tall weeds standing anywhere the gravel didn't hinder growth. There was a slim trail heading out into a field. Becky followed the trail. There was a muddy patch with a small sneaker print indented. She called out more while she walked.

The trail branched out once into the field, two of the directions appeared to settle into the tall weeds, but the third continued into a forest. Sweat dripped down Becky's forehead. Moisture stalled on her arms below the sleeves of an aged t-shirt, bulbs and grains of the tall weeds clung to her skin.

"Jer! Jerrr-em-eee!"

The temperature relented out of the sun's direct touch as Becky stepped into the forest. Annoyance ruled the brunt of her emotions, though worry had begun to poke.

"Jerrr-em-eee!"

"Yeah?"

Not far, behind a fat tree, the boy stood in a soft hole. He looked up at the tree and then to the hole, back and forth.

"You dick breath. You can't go off so far without telling."

"Grandpa's digging stuff."

Becky knew the story of how her grandfather died. If his tools were still there, it probably meant that her brother stood where the old man had croaked.

"Get out of there," Becky said. "Come on, we're going back."

Jeremy didn't argue and climbed out of the hole wearing a suit of filth. He grabbed a small shovel.

"Grandpa's shovel's rotted," he said and tried to heft a pickaxe. It was smaller than normal and the one end came to a broken nub. It was rusty, but Jeremy knew he'd need it, didn't know how or why, but knew. "Can you get one?"

Becky took the pick out of the boy's hand and scooped a spade from the ground.

"All right, dick breath."

"Thanks, butt face."

~

It was around seven, the sun had lost most of its strength but the sky would hold the light for another two hours. A newish black Dodge truck rolled up the dusty driveway.

"I think the Gums are here," Angela said.

Frank stood at the sink. It was his day to do dishes. "Oh good, good." He pulled the plug. The drain gargled.

"There's four of them," Angela said.

"They're farmers?" Jeremy asked.

"Yep. Hey, they've got a daughter too." Frank waved at the window.

Becky saw enough to know that she shouldn't be in a filthy tee and ancient cut-offs. She rushed upstairs to the shower. Nobody noticed her leave.

She'd never had the resources to pull off even imitation high fashion and used stark contrasts to draw attention away from attire. She put her hair in a tight ponytail and began with a light powder to her cheeks and then a dark lip-liner. Then she tossed on a baggy grey t-shirt and tight black jeans.

Becky didn't know if the boy was cute, or smart, or even worth the slight effort she'd made. It was high time she had some love experience and who knew what affect this boy might have on her rep.

Both families had settled on the back porch that overlooked the yard between the house and the main barn. There was a bench along the railing and there was an ancient cast-iron table with flecking white paint. The adults sat at the table. The children, including a woman two months old enough to gamble, sat along the bench. Everyone had a plate.

"They brought pie!" Jeremy shouted, sugary red rhubarb and strawberry filling rimmed his smile like clown lipstick.

"This is Becky," Frank said.

"I'm Sheila, this is Mike, our son Scott, and our daughter Winnie," the mother of the family said. She was frumpy and hardened, like her husband. Winnie was a blank-faced redhead in a light blue summer dress, her hands in her lap holding a dish with a plank-like posture as if there was an etiquette competition happening on the deck.

"Thanks," Becky said, she picked up the pie plate.

There was only one slice remaining and a fork. She plunked down on the bench between her brother and the redhead.

The *adults* discussed community interests. Jeremy and Scott talked about nothing in particular, bouncing from television signal, to sports, to toys, to buried treasure and Arnold Young. Jeremy brimmed with questions and Scott answered what he could.

Winnie rose and offered to take the dishes inside. The door bounced on a spring in her wake.

"She had a boy, he was a couple years older, but we know his folks, and he was a suitable fit. Only rule, she had to wait until she hit eighteen before she run off. She agreed and he agreed. He worked for Royar Feed. There was an accident and for the last three months, poor Winnie's been like a ghost herself. Hasn't even cried yet."

"That's awful, what happened?" Frank asked.

"Her fella was climbing around on a silo. I guess he decided it would take longer to put the harness on than to peek down and carry on with his day. The roof caved around the hole and poor Justin dropped twenty-feet into the corn," Sheila explained.

"That killed him?" Frank was surprised.

"Nope, didn't even have a broken bone when they finally got him out. But you see, the hard thump popped open an access window down below. The corn rushed out and sucked the poor man downwards like a slow cyclone. He breathed corn and that was that."

"That's crazy," Becky said.

Jeremy stared across the deck at the parents, his well of questions dry and a frown on his face. He was imagining what it was like to breath corn.

"That's why, soon as I can, I'm moving far away

from farms. I hear more people die in farm accidents than any other kind of accidents." Scott was suddenly angry, as if his parents risked his life every time they made him go out to do chores.

"Cool your jets," Mike said.

Scott threw his arms into the air and stomped off the deck, Jeremy followed him. Becky waited a few seconds, smiled to the adults and followed along behind the boys. Scott wasn't anything special, but he was a couple years older and that scored some points for him, several points in fact.

"Wait up," Becky called out, jogging to catch up.

The topic had already changed. Moving away from the deck reloaded Jeremy's question bank. Most of it surrounded Arnold Young's digging. Scott tiptoed around the idea that the community thought him nuts. To Scott, living on a farm and doing no farming seemed a pretty good deal.

Becky broke in with a question about the high school.

"Mostly boring knobs doing boring shit."

Becky laughed, unusually girlishly, batting her lashes. Scott caught her signals and promised to look out for her once school started, give her the dirt on her teachers and the others girls in her grade.

"Going into ten, right?" he asked.

She nodded, her eyes holding his.

"Cool, cool," he said, trying to peek down her billowy shirt as the trio stood under a crab apple tree in the front yard near an old cedar rail fence. Becky leaned forward to accommodate his obvious glances.

Oblivious, Jeremy started into questions about his school. Scott switched his gaze and told tall tales of sinister teachers with evil secrets. Jeremy caught on that it was a joke after a while.

Winnie approached from the house. "Mom and Dad want to go now," she said and turned around to walk toward the truck.

"How's your memory?" Scott asked.

"Fine, I guess," Becky said.

"Mine's real good!" Jeremy shouted and then yawned.

It had darkened and the crickets and the black flies were out in full force.

"Then you can help your sister remember. Zero-one-eight-zero, got it?"

"Zero-one-eight-zero!" Jeremy said.

"That you home number?" Becky toed at dirt, eyes downturned.

Scott offered a half smile and a single tip of his chin when she looked up.

~

Bathed and bedded, Jeremy slipped into sleep quickly.

The candlelight was close, but the white stick of wax rested in a brass holder rather than in the palm of Jeremy's recently deceased grandfather. Jeremy picked up the candle and swung it around to peer into the endless black. The flame was much smaller than last time.

"Grandpa?" he whispered and then repeated.

Infinite dark in every direction. He inhaled to ready another call when a sound met his ears. It wasn't his grandfather, but it was something. Jeremy shuffled toward it. Close by, it sounded like whimpering, a child. It took a long time to get a short distance in the dark and he stumbled sightlessly over the uneven ground.

"Grandpa?" he tried again, a little louder.

The whimper continued. Jeremy continued.

A scent rose from the dark. It was earthy like dirt and dog, a little like feces. It encouraged Jeremy. This was a promise of *something* in the vast darkness.

"Grandpa?"

The whimper became a throaty breath. It then whined, like a puppy. Jeremy leaned with the candle and saw large rings of white.

"Shu shu shu, lack!" the whimpering voice screeched and reached out against the white rings.

Jeremy had a dreamer's bravery and leaned closer with the flame. Light glinted off wet eyes from beneath fur and a long snout. It was a like a dog. Sort of. A hand lashed out, trying to grab onto the candle.

Jeremy's eyes widened. The dog's head rode above a sweaty, dark, humanoid body. The creature leapt to its feet in the little cage and Jeremy's gaze roved to its strange genitals. Strings of healed scare tissue sprouted like a bouquet of weeds from what used to be a penis. The bravery faded.

"Shu cack a lack! Rura! Shu shu rura!" the dog creature screamed out, reaching again through its prison bars.

Not bars at all. It was a bone cell, the ribcage of a massive beast. The boy took a step back, shaking his head as if erasing an Etch-a-Sketch.

"Grandpa!"

"There you are!" a familiar voice said.

A palm touched Jeremy's shoulder and the candle dropped, remaining alight on the dark ground. The dog creature whimpered, slinking into the shadows as Arnold Young turned his grandson away.

"What is it?" Jeremy whimpered as he spoke.

"You came early. We were getting ready for you, see?" They walked in the dark until brilliant light flared in the distance. Music joined fireworks. "This is how it is. This is how it can be, forever. It should be this way, don't ya think?"

There were smiling people, clowns, and actors in wonderful animal costumes. There was a stage with marionettes and there were games of chance. It was a carnival, amusement park, circus, sideshow, and theatre rolled into one. They reached a dim ocean-side car chase scene underway. There were cameras and famous people, Jeremy didn't recognize them, but he knew famous people when he saw them. The happy faces had drips of sweat forming and running from their brows.

"Isn't it lovely? All you got to do is find the treasure."

"Where?"

His grandfather smiled and spoke, but no sound came from his mouth.

The bright lights darkened as something crashed against Jeremy's face. He fell, his insides tumbling. There was nothing anywhere, no floor, no ceiling, no crowds, no bone-caged mongrels.

"Grandpa!" He closed his eyes to the darkness.

~

Down the hall, there was a loud bang followed by screeching. Frank and Angela burst from bed where they'd been discussing the neighbor boy and their daughter, and the gaga eyes both wore.

Into Jeremy's room. The boy lay on his back with his arms over his face.

"Jeremy, wake up!" Angela shouted.

"I am awake. There's a monster!"

"Ah, buddy, it's only a—holy shit!" Frank leaned down on the bed while a fat bat dive-bombed.

Angela grabbed at the bat, missed. It crawled over the comforter and onto the boy, looking for chinks in the armour. Frantic, Frank scooped up the bat and threw it against the wall. It thumped and dropped. Angela chased the creature, taking a filthy shirt from the floor, to collect the stunned thing. Frank opened the window and Angela stopped short of releasing it.

Two thoughts: *How did it get in?* and *What about rabies?* The bat remained in the shirt and she rushed to the washroom to drown the intruder.

~

The doctor told them not to worry until they knew they had something to worry about and, *We'll know for sure in the morning.* A nice suggestion, but it defied the nature of worry. It took twenty minutes to get in and out of the hospital.

Jeremy went to bed with his parents. He fell asleep first, dreaming of a skewed real life and awoke thinking that his grandfather's place wasn't so great after all. It was dark and the good stuff was flimsy.

Downstairs, there was a knock.

"You didn't have to come, but I'm sure they'll love the company," Angela said, her voice full of worry.

Earlier that morning, Mike stopped by to go over the property he'd rented. As summer went, it was in the midst of a brief lull that occurred annually. It had rained a few days earlier, the hay was off and baled and the remainder of the crops had, at minimum, a few more days to go before harvest.

It was minutes after six when Mike arrived and close to seven-thirty when he pulled back toward the house. The only trouble he'd found was rocks, but rocks happen and he'd get most of them with the picker attachment come autumn.

Frank caught the man, offered a coffee, and then explained the night before.

That was hours earlier. It was nine-oh-five when Jeremy rolled off the side of his parents' bed and stepped out to see Scott and Winnie.

Winnie forced a smile full of holes. "How ya doing?"

Jeremy frowned and lifted his injured arm. It had three bandages.

"Poor boy," Winnie said.

"Hey, Jeremy," Scott said from behind her.

Upstairs, the shower ran. Frank and Angela were in

the kitchen, Frank tying his shoes, Angela standing over him, waiting. Finished, they stepped toward Jeremy, each taking a turn giving him hugs. He wondered if he did have rabies or maybe mad bat disease.

"I don't know how long we'll be out, but you're free to come or go. Becky's watched him plenty before," Angela said.

"That's okay, better here than home." Scott smiled. It was genuine. "Dad had me painting the barn all day yesterday and I bet he had another exciting day planned for me today."

Angela led the way out. The shower stopped and the sound of the Elfman car rolling away filled the air until it was only silence.

"You hungry?" Scott asked.

"Sure," Jeremy said, "can you make pancakes?"

"I can't, but I bet Winnie can," Scott said. "I can roast weenies and marshmallows and put cereal in bowls, pretty much it."

"I'll make you pancakes," Winnie said.

A door opened upstairs and gentle steps moved slowly downwards. It was Becky. She had a towel over her head and one wrapped around her chest and waist. Jeremy scrunched his face. Before she'd always, always, always dressed in the washroom and then came out. He'd never seen her wear towels.

"Oh, I didn't know you were here."

~

The foursome watched a movie in living room. Becky announced that she was hot and wanted to go outside. Scott seconded the idea.

"Can I come?" Jeremy asked.

Becky suggested that he stay inside for health reasons. "You should play video games, dick breath."

He frowned. He wanted to go with Scott and Becky. Winnie was boring.

Winnie stared at the television, listening, understanding that she'd become an unwanted babysitter.

"Do I got to?"

"Yes, you want to keep it clean and don't itch it," Becky said.

"We'll be back soon enough." Scott followed Becky out of the house.

"Do you want to play one of your games?" Winnie asked.

"Can you even play?" Jeremy pouted, arms folded.

"Maybe, what do you have?" Winnie crouched and looked into the neat stacks in the cabinet under the television. "Hey, I had a *Mario Party* game." For the first time in a long time, she wore an authentic smile over a memory. Mario Party was from before she met Justin, a scar-free time.

"Pfft," Jeremy said. "Fine."

They played for an hour. Jeremy won mostly, but not always. They quit before Winnie really got the hang of things and would have to lose on purpose. She suggested they watch a movie and eat a snack.

The popcorn bowl sat between them, lemonade cups on the table. Jeremy leaned against Winnie. The contact was welcome. For a brief snapshot in her unhappy life, she imagined a life with a child, not her own, she'd snatch one like Jeremy and live out her days as a surrogate mother with no past.

Halfway through *Ninja Turtles*, they both fell asleep, abruptly and simultaneously, sharing a space.

~

Waiting for Jeremy, candle in hand, was Arnold. The flame was tall and bright, and yet only a glint in the vast blackness. Not far away there was a sound and another light. Another candle. Another pair of people.

"Is that Winnie?" Jeremy asked.

"It is. I think she's runnin' into happiness. See, this place is good and happy and that's why you got to dig up the treasure."

"Umm, okay."

"That stupid bat stopped you from listening. The beasts think they own the place, but they don't. It's to share. The old and the new, together. You got to dig under the southeast corner of the basement, there's a spot where the cement's weak and crumbling," Arnold said.

Overhead a large bird-like creature squawked, "Shu shu, oob a la lack, shu shu!"

Jeremey ducked, seeing only the shape. It was like a crow, but massive with a smooth round head and a long spiked tail.

"I don't like these things," Jeremy whispered when he was certain the bird was gone.

"Don't worry. There's not so many animals and we'll try and leave them behind when we come."

"I don't know. It's scary, Grandpa."

"Nope, your perception gettin' in the way."

"Oh." Jeremy didn't understand and didn't want to.

"Mind me now."

~

On the fleeting tail of a bang, the darkness evaporated into pinkness. Jeremy opened his eyes and looked at Winnie and then over to the other couch, to Becky and Scott. They both blushed, guilt written in the creases around their eyes.

For the first two hours, they'd walked. Scott finally got up the nerve to hold her hand, then he kissed her and the juices flowed. Scott was prepared to stop whenever Becky said.

Becky was down to boogie.

Becky and Scott cast away their virginities on an act lasting three seconds longer than eight minutes.

Winnie did not look at them. Her eyes burrowed into Jeremy. "Are you going to dig?" Tears bubbled. "You have to find it."

"What?" Scott said.

"You have to dig, okay? Justin said you knew where to dig."

Jeremy nodded. He rose from the couch and shuffled outside to gather the borrowed tools.

"What's going on?" Becky asked.

Winnie looked at the pair, knew the look, heard a tidbit in the dark place. "You should wear a condom next time. If he doesn't dig, I'll tell everyone what you did."

Becky's lips tightened and Scott scowled.

It shouldn't matter anyway, the kid liked digging. The sound of the storm cellar door opening and closing blared over the tense living room.

It shook Scott into sense. "We didn't do nothing. Besides, she's my girlfriend."

Becky's heart melted. She'd never been a girlfriend and after that step she took a leap, someday they'd marry and have children, buy a house.

"You fucked her under a pine tree," Winnie said, her voice powerful and willful, nothing like it had been hours earlier. "He will dig and you will help him when I can't," she said to Becky.

"Why?"

"Shut your mouth, your breath smells slutty. If you don't want shit for doing what you did, you'll help your brother."

A car rolled along the lane and a dust cloud followed. Frank and Angela stepped into view, all smiles.

"We're home!" Frank announced. "And Jer doesn't have rabies!"

The stare-down continued in the living room, but only between brother and sister. Becky worried that her parents would smell sex. She burst off.

"Got to pee," she called out behind her.

"What a weirdo," Angela said. "We stopped by your house. Your parents want you home."

Winnie nodded and stepped past her brother. "Goodbye," she said from the door.

"I guess we're going. Ding-ding, bring in the slave labor." Scott was visibly angry. "Bye Becky!" he shouted up the stairs. "See ya later," he added to the Elfman parents.

"That was strange," Angela said after she heard the Gums' old Jeep engine start.

"And what is that?" Frank looked to the door to the basement.

Above, the toilet flushed accompanying the tink-tink-tink coming from below.

They followed the louder sound and got halfway down the stairs before they saw Jeremy. The basement was damp and musty, mostly empty. There were old flood lines on the whitewashed stone and the appliances lived on brick stilts. Jeremy was in a corner, there were a few baseball-sized hunks of old cement tossed aside and he worked at digging up a stony swatch.

"What are you doing?" Angela said.

"Digging."

"We can see that, do you plan on digging up the whole basement?" Angela asked.

"No."

"Well, stop!"

Jeremy did not stop.

"You know it's probably not a big deal. We'll need to find the leaks eventually. Maybe he's digging with luck. Be careful buddy." Frank was too happy to harbor negative thoughts.

"I didn't consider that." Angela let the light-heartedness come back to the surface, *no rabies, no biggie.* "Next, go ahead and dig us a pool in the backyard, would ya?"

Jeremy didn't answer. He didn't want them to see him crying. It was hard to explain about dreams that were more than dreams. He knew they wouldn't understand.

~

It was the third day in a row that Winnie had come to visit with Jeremy. She said she liked being around him and that it helped her think of something other than lost love. Angela thought it reasonable and Frank thought it harmlessly odd.

Jeremy and Winnie were in the basement. Becky and Scott were in the living room. Angela and Frank were in the backyard. The entire family had had terrible sleeps, nightmares kept them awake after brief stints of rest. The subject matter went unspoken and none had any idea that they all dreamed of the same black world like a void that moved infinitely toward more nothingness.

It was the afterlife. There was no heaven. There was only punishment for having lived at all.

"Lemonade?" Frank asked.

He'd lain in the shade while Angela lied on her back, soaking up radiation.

"Sure, but I'll come in with you."

Frank helped Angela to her feet. They stepped inside.

The cellar opened next to the deck and Winnie's voice rose up the steps. "Where are you going?"

Jeremy ran past and got to the living room. He needed Scott. The only remedy for a troublesome sister is a brother.

"Keep her away," he whispered, sounding much older than he was. He then turned to Becky. "Start a fire."

"What?"

"She'll bring the black," Jeremy said.

Scott hadn't a clue, didn't need one, his sister had really pissed him off lately and he wanted to put her in her place. She was only nineteen months older than he was. Becky, however, understood fear of that blackness, or rather, an abyss, a vacuum of the light, she understood the terror of shadows. She'd dreamed demons and beasts, and dead people that lived in perfect horrible darkness. They hungered to devour the light of the world.

"Did you find it?" Winnie asked.

"What the hell, Winnie?" Angela had hands on hips.

Everyone stood in the living room staring at the distraught girl.

"Let's go, sis. You're being crazy." Scott grabbed her arm and she cocked back a fist and slugged him in the jaw.

He hadn't expected the strike and dropped, but bounced upright like an inflatable punching bag. He pounced and smothered her.

"Hey, knock it off!" Frank shouted.

Jeremy ran back toward the door to the basement and stopped briefly to look at Becky. "Fire!" He tore down the stairs, Angela chasing after him.

Becky broke for the woodshed attached to the carport and gathered the paper recyclables from the bin, kindling from the ancient woodpile, and matches from the spider-webby ledge. There was a small fire pit in the backyard for roasts and camp outs, they always used it whenever they'd visited before Arnold died. She dumped the paper and cardboard into the pit and built a teepee of kindling.

There were screams and shouts inside, glass breaking, and furniture tumbling. Becky knocked the kindling askew. Imperfection mattered none, she lit a flyer for the Super-Value grocery and the flames licked slowly and then died from a lack of oxygen within the stacked materials. A door slammed behind her and Jeremy yelled.

"Fire, fire!"

He had a pale white book in his hands. The boy was filthy, but the book was spotless. It looked like a smooth new alabaster baby puled fresh from a milk bath. It seemed eerily like human flesh. She kneeled and lit the paper again. It was damp from the mugginess and refused to stay lit.

Jeremy tossed the book into the pit. There was a mouth on the front, a long pink tongue stretched, licking lip-less edges. It smacked as if freshly awoken. Becky screamed, while she made a third attempt at lighting the paper. It caught on the oldest cardboard, though weakly. Winnie shouted from inside.

"Burn it!" Tears streaked Jeremy's dusty cheeks.

An image flashed before Becky's mind and she rushed to the small shed. There was a red can sitting next to a greasy Stihl chainsaw. The can was half-full and she lugged it back to the pit, the contents sloshing and misting out the breather hole where a yellow cap hung by a plastic tether, unscrewed.

The fire continued to burn, barely charring the kindling. The book's cover hardly browned, the mouth sneered. Becky twisted the cap off, slowing to a trot. The cap fell into the grass and she dumped the mixed gasoline over the fire, dousing the petering flames.

"No!" Winnie ran out toward the pit. Her face was puffy and bloody.

Scott chased behind her, looking even worse. Frank behind him. Angela stood where she had since Jeremy ran outside. She was in awe of the book as it made her think of the impossible dream. That mouth carried the same vacant emptiness. That mouth was a window into abyss.

Winnie dived through the shower of gasoline and oil

to rescue the book. A flicker from beneath the cardboard found the vapors and celebrated in a hot ball nine shades of orange.

The flames leapt onto Winnie. She straitened and screamed, and yet, managed to open the book. The tongue stretched and licked her knuckles. The leathery pages, script written in the sacrificial blood, were a way to requite love.

"Shu ca, rura, shu!" she read.

Jeremy cried into his palms. He was done. It was over.

"Shu shu, la loo ka shu!"

The flames bubbled Winnie's flesh and she fell to her knees.

"Winnie!" Scott shouted, after the initial shock passed, he jumped on his sister. The fire burned him and he rolled away from the pain.

"Scott, no." Becky leapt onto Scott to drown the flames dancing over his t-shirt.

"Sool kylatooyo, shu shu, shu shu, la loo ka rura," Winnie mumbled, the fumes rode her inhalation and lit her tongue and throat. She managed to flip the page. "Huu shu shu, la loo ka." Her skin was of red scales and open sores below the flames.

The mouth on the book quoted on the tail of the words spoken, as if taking an oath, its voice inaudible.

Frank ran with a blanket that he'd retrieved from the woodshed. He tossed it on Winnie. Becky and Scott stopped rolling and stared at the smoke rising from the smoldering body beneath the blanket.

"No more," Jeremy whined. He dropped down next to the alight pit. Frank picked him up and stepped back.

"Is she…?" Angela didn't want to say it.

There were holes and superficial burns on Scott's hands, arms, and chest. He crawled toward his sister. Becky wished she had the strength to join him, but she didn't, and watched him go.

"Winnie?" he whispered. He didn't want to touch her and hurt her further. There was a wheeze and he put his ear next to the outline of her head.

"Ka la loo, sepow a dim, shu shu, rura, rura, shu shu," the small voice wheezed.

"Winnie?" He chanced a gentle nudge and the ground began to shake beneath her body.

Scott stumbled in a backwards crab crawl. Winnie teetered and then slid down into a hole as it chewed through the lawn. Blackness sucked up the light directly over the hole and a loud screech called out. All but Scott recognized the voices of the beasts from the dark.

"What the fuck?" Scott said.

Instinctively, the Elfman family backpedaled, away from the pure budding void, away from the beam of impenetrable vacancy that grew into the sky.

"Shu shu!" a voice screeched and two thumps sounded from below. A hoof-footed man with a peaked head and a mouth that opened like an accordion leaned over Scott. It roared triumph.

Scott turned to crawl and the black accordion mouth opened wide to bite. A clean amputation of everything below the waist. Becky screamed. Angela grabbed her, turning away.

"Run to the car, go," Frank said. His family led the way as he stumbled in reverse, unwilling to withdraw his gaze, a manoeuvre he'd heard worked with brown bears.

More blackness ate the light and three more creatures climbed topside. Two men with mutilated bodies and dog heads, flesh yellowy white. The third was a bird, a black ostrich with a head of serrated spaghetti tentacles, hundreds of tiny reaching appendages.

Up the lane, the Gums' Dodge rolled toward the house. Frank forwent his staring contest and got into the front seat next to Angela. She barked the car alive.

"Drive! Drive!" Frank screamed.

"I am! Don't yell at me!" Angela tore out the laneway, veering into a field as she passed the red truck.

Frank watched in the mirror. At first, the Dodge stopped and then it moved on. The blackness ate the collapsing barn and then the shed, creeping outward in every direction, rising high into the air and *beyond*.

Watching no more, the Elfman's Nissan pulled out onto the road.

~

They drove into the night and through the following day, stopping at automated pumps for fuel and then at drive-thru restaurants for meals. Becky's iPod rolled through a playlist of upbeat pop absurdity. The bouncing rhythms and lyrics clashed against the blank shock. They'd made it halfway across the country when they finally stopped for a sleep break.

They'd heard nothing of the void, but hadn't been listening for it. It was a bad dream so long as they ignored it.

The four of them slept on two beds, husband and wife, brother and sister. They dreamed brief snippets of bright, modified reality. They awoke feeling better, they'd overreacted, knowing the blackness was only over the farm and, surely, the army killed everything stepping forth.

"Morning," Frank said as he fixed a pot of coffee in the tiny percolator on top of a mini fridge.

"Morning," the trio said back one after another.

The machine bubbled and Frank sat down on the bed. "What do you think?"

"It was bad, but I'm sure it's over," Angela said. "Maybe I'll paint the creatures, maybe they are my singular thought, maybe it was my imagination manifesting itself."

Frank leaned over and kissed her. Becky lied flat while Jeremy sprang up and leapt onto his mother before breaking for the washroom. It was a dull morning through the small window above the toilet. Wonderful greyness.

There was hope left in greyness. "Is it better?" Jeremy asked, kicking the door closed before plopping down onto the can.

"Has to be. I tried to check the TV, but the cable's out," Frank said, speaking to the closed door.

Jeremy heard only a grumble as he pushed out the road food turned to pasty mush. The door was heavy. He sure hoped it was better. Finished he ran the water to wash his face. He closed his eyes. Panicked, his eyelids rebelled against the absence of light and he turned to the window. The light still existed. He would never take it for granted again.

The tap water coughed and rushed. Jeremy continued washing until every smoke streak was gone from his cheeks. He opened the door. "Are we going—?" The words caught in his throat as he peered at the midnight wall and the sickening black creatures on top of his family, crimson geysers sprouted from throats and torn limbs; undead, each wore silent horror masks, seeping fluids drained the pigment of their flesh.

Angela looked across the room at Jeremy and with a bloody, gargling voice said, "Shu shu, rura shu shu. Shu shu forever."

Three short creatures, like humans, but scaly-skinned with vulture beaks, hopped off the bed and approached Jeremy. Their shadows ate light. The boy closed and locked the door. He stared out the window and prayed for the strength of light, despite the quick casting shadow dimming the hues.

Out there, nightmarish eagles squawked with raspy tongues, "Shu shu, rura cack a lack! Shu shu!"

Jeremy gazed into the grey beyond the shaking glass. "Shu shu forever."

For hundreds of miles in every direction, night ate day and was only getting started.

Slithering

A small boy pointed an orange laser pistol at his sister. He squeezed the trigger. A spinning light flashed as the kazoo-like sound zipped. The sister fell, thrashing on the sunbaked asphalt amid the mysterious fluid stains, the faded black rubber marks, and the reflective specks of long-ago shattered glass.

"Get up. You'll get dirty and then you'll have to explain to your father why he doesn't have a good daughter that stays clean and minds her manners," a woman said. She had a square face and wore a baby blue shorts and vest combination, featuring a matching hat with a wide brim. Plastic bangles in a rainbow of shades jangled at the wrists.

The shot daughter stood up as told, but being good was somebody else's business. She pulled a pink laser pistol from behind her back. "You die now, doody brains." She squeezed and the light flashed while the weapon roared its zipping cry.

The boy, the brother, the doody brains, took the shot and stumbled. Like any brother playing a game of imagination, succumbing to his sister is not the objective. He did not fall.

"I shot you, pee face!" sister screamed and squeezed again.

There was mugginess on the air. Stagnant around the hazy gasoline atmosphere.

"You two, behave!" The mother started around the side of her long Cadillac Seville. She wore brown leather sneakers, sensible mom shoes, beneath the too blue outfit.

The boy groaned and grunted, the invisible laser beams filled him with action. He began shaking, moaning, tongue out, a full-fledged standing seizure, grandstand mal. Slowly his arm rose and the orange laser pistol pointed at girl.

"I shot you, dink, doodie, pee brains!" The third kazoo siren called out and before the boy could squeeze in retaliation. He stumbled backward. There he was, dead on his feet, the victim of imaginary intergalactic pistols at dawn.

His body continued beyond the acting point and slammed with a thump into the side of a silver Chevrolet Cruze.

"Michael, you little—I'm so sorry about that. His father's in the hospital and they're just acting out, the little shits. I think they're scared," the mother said.

"Am not!" the boy, doody brains, pee face, dink shouted as he rose from the side of the Chevy. The steel body thumped outward in thanks, contours jumping into uniform. The magic of conglomerating plastics with steel.

The address brought Kaci Moonie out of a thoughtful trance, back down from memory lane's reverie. Seeing the brother and sister and the woman in her baby blue outfit—easy and affordable fashion for moms the world over—carried with it a flashback.

It might've been a false memory or it might've been a hint into a life forgotten. She saw herself and a boy with a finger gun, outside a similarly bleached gas station. There was a mother in a lime green jumper and python print sandals. High quality fakes. The woman called to her, *Eve, you'll dirty your Sundays.*

Kaci smiled at the real-time mother. "No worries, it's a rental."

The woman nodded and then gathered her family. The glass door littered with ice cream, potato chip, and energy drink advertisements opened and a steel bell jangled. Adam Coots stepped out wearing a curious frown. His eyes followed the Cadillac as it rolled away from the lot before settling back on his fiancé.

He'd attempted to explain the importance of retaining approval from his parents, but mostly the explanation failed to manifest into anything more than blabbering. Kaci didn't mind, this was a show of empathy on her part. The kind of understanding that suggested a workable future, a long one.

To ease the strain he put on himself, she'd attempted to explain how she didn't truly understand, but wanted to understand. Families, real families, were a subject you learned easiest firsthand. Otherwise, it was important to be open and subjective.

To Adam one family was like another, mostly, and he smiled as if to suggest, *what's to understand, they're all weird.*

Given up at the age of four, Kaci's adopting parents divorced and she began a steady bounce. New girlfriends and wives, new boyfriends and husbands. In and out of homes until college. She appreciated Adam's need to keep his family happy because she didn't have anything left of her real family. Sometimes when she longed to know her past, she ran a gentle touch over the aged and stretched ovular scare tissue on her wrist.

This was from her first life, the life before adoption. She knew this because neither faux-parent placed blame of the mark on the other faux-parent. Old times, a mark of mystery, the period that fluttered the first fixed memories. Still, tidbits lapped at the shore now and then, topics laced and littered with information connecting reality and potential for imagination.

Since when are memories trustworthy anyway?

"Ready to go?" Adam asked as he rubbed an absent touch to his forehead.

"That bite still bothering you?" Kaci pulled the pump nozzle from the tank. The pump's computer printed out a receipt while she screwed the plastic cap into place.

"Yeah, I feel like it's growing. Probably stop growing if I could stop touching it. I can't. I'm trying not to touch it at all. It's like have a canker on my face."

Kaci imagined Adam reaching a long tongue to his forehead as she snatched the receipt from the pump.

"Do you really think your parents will like me?"

"How could they not?" he said and started the car. It was so quiet that he'd double jogged the ignition twice since leaving the airport parking lot.

"Umm, I blurt out horrible things when we hump," she said.

He smiled and shook his head.

She continued, "Oh, sometimes if I eat too much cheese I get really gross gas. I'm impatient with stupid people and yet, I obsess over affluent dullards that make sex tapes and give their children directions or numbers for names. Oh god, they're not like Trump supporters, are they?"

"I doubt it, to them all politics aside from their own is devil business. No, they're just... besides, you're no different in that stuff. I mean cheese can give anybody gas." Adam reached over and squeezed her knee as he drove. "Granted, your ass does have a way with poison that Mengele would commend."

"Adam!"

He took his hand back. "Sorry, that was the wrong kind of funny. But seriously, cool it, okay? They'll like you. You're very likeable."

Outside the window was a world of trees and little else. A crow perched on a high branch staring down at a seagull picking at something in the ditch. More trees. Another crow. More trees. A rabbit hopped into the long grass and out of view. More trees.

"Fine, but what about animals. They hate me, only cats and Jody's pot-bellied pig put up with me."

"No, remember that African thing at the zoo?"

Kaci rolled her eyes. They'd gone to the San Francisco Zoo while visiting the city for a week. In a glassed-in viewing area, an entire family of small animals followed her along the glass, stopping when she did, scooting along to catch up when she moved, and whining when she left.

"Right, how could I forget the badger thingies?"

"Meerkats, weren't they?"

"No, it was something else. Who cares? What I remember were those monkeys. Remember the monkeys?" Kaci reached along his thigh and squeezed the tip of his dick. The monkeys had been frantic, horny with action.

"Hey, get out of here." Adam slapped her hand.

Kaci retracted her touch. "Okay, but I need to know. So stop changing the subject. You never want to talk about them and in two hours, I'm going to meet them, so spill."

He took a deep breath. "I'm sorry, honey. I don't know what you mean."

"Fine," she said in a pout, but quickly regained focus. "Let's play a game. I'll tell you something funny about my mom and you tell me something funny about your mom, deal?"

Adam remained quiet.

"Deal?"

"Fine."

Kaci began. Her mother for the purposes of her stories was her faux-mother. Only in her head did the term faux-mother mean anything, outwardly, she put the old times away. Things of thought, not expression. "So when I was really small, I doodled because I saw my mom doodle on things. All of her doodles were of animals. In her planner, on pizza boxes, in the telephone book, and anywhere else boredom met blank space. No big deal.

"In the second grade we had to supply our own workbooks. I'd filled mine with my name. I was so proud of my smooth printing that I covered every page with Kaci Leila Moonie. It was only a month into school, so I needed another workbook and I thought my mom would be upset about the wastefulness, or something. She used to get pissy about things, all things. Anyway, so I started looking around in the basement for paper I could staple into my booklet and I found a box of my mom's college stuff. I found binders loaded with paper. I pulled them out and her familiar animals were in the corners of most of the pages, but they were different.

"Every single horse, monkey, cat, dog, pig, elephant, and lizard had a tiny penis. No balls, just a tiny baby penis for every animal. Ha!"

"Then what?" Adam either missed the humor or sought to delay his turn with the metaphorical conch.

"Itsy-bitsy penises are funny, although I didn't think it at the time. I yelled at her and tried to relay a message my teacher gave to some the boys in class that wrote in textbooks. She got really mad at me and then feeling stupid about, I think, took me shopping for more school supplies. It's not really the point. The point is the tiny penises were something funny my mom did. Now your turn." Kaci was nearly out of breath when she finished.

"Is your mother a pervert?"

"No more than me! Now your turn, something small and funny."

Adam grimaced. "Fine."

"Let's hear it."

"Fine! When I was a kid, I used to bowl in the league in town. My parents would drop me off and I'd go in and play games with the other kids. I'd gotten pretty good and in my third season, I was on the Rockets. Every year the league manager mixed up the teams based on how good or bad players were the year before, and if there were any new players, he sprinkled them throughout.

"Like I said, I was on the Rockets and we were in the semi-finals and my parents finally decided they'd come to watch a game. I saw them at the start, they waved and then I didn't see them again until after I'd finished my final frame. I was good, but not the best, so my third set of throws was the ninth. The score was close and then the last boy on the other team, the Grizzlies, got up and threw. A boy on my team nudged me with a smile. A finger guided my sightline to a pair of weirdoes with their faces planted on the floor, sliding around every time the pins crashed.

"I thought I would die. It was my parents and there was my mother in her stupid snakeskin purse and my dad in his filthy work boots sliding around the floor feeling the vibrations or something. They're freaks in public, at home it wasn't so weird… or, I guess I didn't know any better."

"Oh god, that's fucking crazy. What did you do?"

"I ran. I found out at school that we won and then next weekend the Rockets beat the Giant Spruces for the championship, even down a player. I had to hear it at school. I haven't bowled since."

"Christ, that's nuts." Kaci suddenly understood why her fiancé avoided vocalizing his past. Still, they were to marry and she was about to meet these people.

"I know."

"Are they like wacko hippies? Were they getting energy from the floor?"

"Something."

Adam fell silent as Kaci mulled it over. Her eyes returned to the outdoors. "You still owe me a funny one. That was just sad and weird. I bet kids made fun of you."

"No, never. Nobody said a word. The kid that nudged me was homeschooled, so I guess he was the only one that didn't recognize my parents. I think people were afraid of my family."

"Okay, now you've got to tell me everything. I mean Jeeesus."

Adam stared forward and focussed on the road.

"Not gonna offer a nugget for free? I get ya. We'll go like Hannibal and Clarice, we'll make the *lambs scream.*

"I have a sad one I've never told anybody but my mom. After my parents divorced, they both jumped into new relationships. Well, my dad had been secretly with his girlfriend for months and my mom wanted an even score. She started dating this guy from her work. I don't know how it started. He was with the security company that did stuff at her office I guess.

"Anyway, they'd been together for months and I kept jumping back and forth between Mom and Dad. And one day, Gary, the security guy, was there and my mom said he was going to spend the night. No big deal, he slept over and it was fine. We played Clue and then I had a bath and went to bed.

"In the middle of the night I got up because I heard something funny in the living room. The sound was super weird at the time. I had to be quiet in case it was my mom because she'd order me right away back to bed. It wasn't my mom. It was Gary, and he was watching television and shaking. I only saw his silhouette around the light from the video on the screen.

"All through school we had teachers telling us right and wrong and to tell someone if there was something that made us feel bad. So I ran to my mom's bedroom when I saw myself on the screen. Gary had a hidden camera in the bathroom and filmed my bath time. I was nine."

"Holy crow, that's sick! I'm so sorry that happened to you." Adam wore a valid expression, even if the bath time thing could've been so much worse. "That's disgusting. What did your mother do?"

"I whispered the story to her and she sat up and whispered back to me and I repeated, *Gary's watching me in the tub and I'm naked*. She didn't understand, but she got up and flicked the light switch in the living room and Gary jumped up started and tried to yank up his pants. The goof fell down on the coffee table. He'd finished, the proof was all over a washcloth he'd used as a catcher's mitt.

"Mom chased him out of the house and made me promise never to tell my father or I'd never get to see her again. I promised. I know it should probably bother me, but it doesn't. I kind of feel sorry for Gary."

"How, how could you possibly feel sorry for some pervert watching child pornography?" There was fury in the question.

"I doubt Gary would watch child porn if it wasn't what he was attracted to, people don't choose what they love. They just love it and it sucks for people that love the wrong things. Once you get over some great god law of masterful design, you're left with the true imperfect things and the imperfect things they do. We're like monkeys escaped from the zoo."

"So you think your mother's boyfriend should be allowed to record children in the bathtub?"

"Hell no! That's not what I said. I said I feel sorry for Gary because what he loves is wrong and hurts people. He's probably in prison or hurting someone and I bet he feels guilty, or at least he should feel guilty." Kaci's gaze had returned to Adam's face as he stared forward. The bump on his head had grown since the gas station. "Tons of people fight impulses all the time. Gary was an adult, there is no reason he couldn't control impulses." Kaci paused, then said, "That thing on your forehead is getting worse."

Adam's fingers explored with ginger touch. "Maybe it's a stress bump, a manifestation of you meeting my parents."

"It doesn't matter." Kaci patted Adam's knee. "We won't be making this trip often, will we?"

He shook his head.

"See, no biggie. Your turn, you owe me a funny story about your parents."

He inhaled and exhaled in a huff. "All right," he said and trailed off, smirked, then resumed, "When I was small we lived in a private community. I think it had to do with church or Jesus. This was before we moved to the farm.

"Our community had this tradition where we settled with ourselves for one month, like no outside contact at all. I think it was supposed to be a cleansing thing. A one-month commune vacation without leaving home. I was eight and it was the quiet month, October, and Dad went out to the shed every night. He said he had some huge project that needed finishing. I don't remember what it was supposed to be because he wasn't building anything.

"Now my mother was serious, mega serious about the

month off, and she didn't care that it was October and didn't know a thing about baseball."

Kaci laughed recognizing where the story led. She and Adam were the same age. October, when they were eight, was also the same October the Toronto Blue Jays flew into Atlanta and left with the World Series Championship in pocket. Kaci grew up just outside Toronto and Adam grew up in southeastern Georgia.

"As a kid, I took *the word* as truth, every story my parents and the pastor drove home from the community's version of the Bible. I believed there was a Hell, like real fire and torture Hell, for anyone not following the rules.

"I went out to the shed to ask my father a question and there he was, disobeying the rules of the community and God. I rushed back to the house to tell my mother that Satan had my father. She raged and stomped outside. She always wore something in snakeskin, shoes, belt, purse, always at least one thing, usually more. For years, she had these cowboy boots of black and green skin. She wore those as she stomped out of the house in her underwear and a t-shirt. I thought for sure my father was a dead man. I thought she'd kill him and cook him for supper and his soul was about to shoot right down to Hell.

"She got to the window and I think he saw her shadow or sensed her fury because he shot to his feet and instead of yelling at him, she turned away. I followed her out onto the gravel road and down to where the pastor lived."

Adam shook his head and smiled at the thought. "She charged into the pastor's house and started into a tirade, my father was outside, catching up, calling for her to stop, begging her. My mother quit shouting. I was so scared about what the pastor was going to do. I think in most cases the penalty for disobeying the laws was a shunning, a big deal in small communities. But the pastor was quiet and Don Sutton was in the air, explaining through the pastor's tiny radio that John Smoltz had to face Roberto Alomar to start things off in the top-half."

Kaci clapped. "Ha! That's great, then what happened?"

Adam frowned. "We moved a month later. My mother thought the whole community was full of liars and heathens. I never liked the farm, but at least I got to go to regular school and take science classes."

Kaci looked out the window again as a memory fluttered. This one seemed more false than most, her imagination piecing together the old time before with bits of Adam's story. She saw herself and a man in a shed full of cages, cheering on voices from a portable TV. The man had a lumpy head and dark yellow eyes.

She shivered at the image. "How much longer?"

"An hour yet." Adam absently fingered the bump on his forehead that had become something of a nub. "Your turn to tell a story."

"You've met my parents, it isn't the same."

"I met them once and your mother was drunk and your father was busy trying to pick-up the college girls."

Kaci sniggered. "They were both drunk, I'll have you know. I don't think they'd seen each other for close to a decade. One of the nannies always dropped me off for visitations. Also, what grown man can turn blind to young women in graduation robes? Super sexy, right? Maybe he's really into bright minds."

At the time she did not find her parents amusing, in fact she found them both painfully embarrassing. Dwelling on the past had gone rotten. She had a few extra tidbits and pushing Adam too much never worked. Instead of forcing chatter, she increased the volume on the radio and averted her gaze back out the window as the airwave friendly rock, pop, and R&B songs filled the car.

Kaci leaned her forehead against the window. Tree after tree zoomed past in green and brown blurs. There were crows and gulls, some roadkill, and ditch trash, but little else to look at. Suddenly, as if dropped from the sky, the trees stopped and asphalt and cement filled her vision.

"Hey, is this the town where you went to school?"

She turned to Adam as she asked. He rubbed at the nub. It had grown more. His eyes had reddened and his cheeks paled.

"Yes," he whispered.

"You can't be that nervous, are you?"

He remained quiet.

"Come on, talk to me."

He cleared his throat. "I haven't been home in so long."

Kaci rubbed his leg. "I know, but—"

"No! You don't know. When I went off to college they told me they never wanted to see me again. They told me I wasn't one of them and that I was a disappointment to them, and to God. You don't know what it means to me that they called. Remember we did the cards and I did my parents' without you. I told them all about you and how we would be married and I really wanted their blessing and that I miss them." A few tears rolled down Adam's cheeks as he spoke. "I knew you wouldn't understand about that since your parents—"

Something snapped in Kaci. "I wouldn't understand? My parents basically tossed me away. I don't even know who they are! I miss the idea of real parents just as much as you miss your freaks!"

Neither spoke for close to a minute.

Nickelback's Chad Kroger moaned a motivational ballad about following dreams and Kaci broke into laughter. The rental cleared the final bits of town and resumed the treeline view.

"What's so funny?"

"Nothing… everything. We are, your parents, Nickelback, the ninety-two Blue Jays and Braves, your bowling team, Gary, all of this. We're bound to fail if we don't loosen up about life." Kaci leaned over and kissed Adam. "Also, once we're back in the city, you're getting that bump checked out."

"Damn right I am. I thought it was a bug bite or a jumbo pimple or something, but, holy moley is it big."

Kaci laughed again. "Holy moley?"

"Getting into the swing, my parents are deeply religious and swearing is not a good idea. My mother rammed soap bars into my mouth until I was seventeen and she only stopped because I left."

"Holy Christ. I mean holy moley."

Adam smiled. He wheeled the car from the pale two-lane highway onto a pale gravel road barely wide enough for two opposing automobiles, should they roll with their right-hand wheels in the grass. No traffic approached for the four-minute trip to the farm.

"Here we are," Adam said, his voice was shaky.

Kaci gazed out to the wide-open space, the tall farmhouse, the small shed, the red barn in need of a paint job. She wanted to ask if there was a rule about red barns, a Biblical law perhaps, but she didn't. The laneway was a little better than a half-kilometre and as they drew closer, both Adam and Kaci soaked in the ill repair of the place.

"Did it always look like this?" Kaci asked.

Adam shook his head and parked in front of the shed. He kicked open the door and hit the trunk release. "Oh, one thing. I'm about ninety-nine percent sure of it, but I'll bet we're sleeping in separate rooms. We'll pretend that's normal and—"

"Pretend that we haven't bathed each other like kitty cats or that sometimes you like me to suck you off and put my fingers in—?"

"Cripes, enough," Adam said. It wasn't funny and the nub on his forehead throbbed, verging toward unbearably.

"I'm sorry. I'll behave, but it'll cost you when we get back."

Adam ignored her and hopped out of the rental. Both started toward the trunk. They each had a small suitcase, Kaci thought it strange when they packed, but now understood it. Two suitcases was part of the ruse, the good Christian boy routine.

"Hey, what kind of church are they anyway?" Kaci followed her future husband toward his childhood home.

"Uh, was Pentecostal I think, but they pray from home. They did last I knew, it's a little weird. The old church, I mean, the community one. It broke up for legal reasons a few years after we left."

"Wait," Kaci stopped, "why didn't you get into this in the car?"

"I kind of hoped we'd crash, I think. Nothing serious, just that we'd never get here. I'm so nervous—"

"Yeah, fine, but what about your parents, it's not like really scary stuff, just embarrassing, right?"

Adam turned to face the house. He couldn't look at Kaci when he said it. "My parents are snake-handlers. I was a snake-handler growing up."

"Fuck off," Kaci whispered.

"No swearing, come on. It's not as if they keep snakes in the house."

Paint, chipped and peeling in long oblong strands, revealed greyed wood beneath the outer coats. Kaci glanced over Adam's shoulder wondering if he should open the door that he must've opened about a million times, or simply knock. There was a note and he did neither.

Gone for night. Emergency out of town, make yourself and your friend at home. We will be back in the morning. Spare bed made up in sewing room.

"Weird. They must've joined a new church or gotten in contact with the old family… crazy."

"Why do you say that?"

"You can't have an emergency out of town unless you know someone out of town. My father has brothers, but they hadn't talked since my mother and father went away. So he'd said, but that was like a million years ago."

"Shall we? We can get all the swears and doing it out of our system," Kaci joked.

Adam looked up at the stern and harsh house, built on laws and order, God's word and Satan's promises. The idea of defying the rules of the house gave giddy caterpillars in his belly the power to transform and flutter. He opened the door and held out a hand so that Kaci could enter first.

He leaned in to whisper as she stepped by. "I'm gonna fuck your brains out."

Eyes bulged with anticipation as she brushed by, rubbing her ass on the front of his pants. Adam followed her inside. It started in the kitchen, the table and floor, and moved into the dining room, on the hardwood first, but then rolling about the thick knit rug. Finally stripped fully, they made for the living room and Adam's eyes swelled as he erupted into Kaci's wet chasm after twenty minutes of sweaty pumping.

Kaci raised from the couch, a brown corduroy monster from sometime in the seventies, and stepped toward her strewn underwear, her thighs roughened and sticky.

"What are you doing?" Adam asked.

Kaci looked back and saw Adam had his cock in his

hand, glistening, attempting to ready himself for a round two. Furiously, he slid the conglomeration of his fluid and her fluid along the shaft and over the bulbous head.

"Aren't we a little home-front horn doggy?"

"To the upstairs!" Adam led and Kaci chased behind him, naked, jiggling, and free of worry.

They started in Adam's boyhood bedroom, moved then to the sewing room and the washroom. With a moan and a splash, they fell back sweaty and raw. Kaci sat on the can while Adam remained on the floor, her bangs clung to her forehead as if she'd climbed out of the pool, but she didn't smell of chlorine. Instead, the fishy primordial scent coated them both like rejected perfume attempts.

She stood up. "Shower?"

He rubbed at the nub on his forehead. It was growing again. "Yeah sure, but there's one more room."

"What?" Kaci thought all the sex was great, but by the end, she'd begun to dry out on rub of things gone on long enough.

"Don't worry," he said as if reading her mind. "We'll go slow."

"Who are you?" Kaci started the shower.

After a dutiful wash, Adam took Kaci's hand and led her to his parents' bedroom. The house possessed him with urgent need, he had to affront the past and cause the equivalent trouble he should've as a child, even if nobody would ever know.

Kaci lay back on the made bed. Adam crawled up between her legs and started a slow methodical tongue treatment. As much as they'd washed, he still tasted himself, vaguely, alongside her blooming glaze.

Looking about her while embracing the familiar lapping, rimming, pushing, Kaci scanned for photos or paintings, hoping for the small town kitsch she saw sometimes at flea markets. On the wall at the end of the bed was a Jesus with his arms out and palms up as if catching raindrops. Snakes wound his hands, shoulders, and neck. The image sent a shiver through her body and Adam took it as a sign that he'd hit something. He attacked without much success.

"My turn," Kaci said and they traded spots.

He'd gotten hot dog hard but no more. Firm but without the essential bone for boning. Kaci snuggled next to him. They napped until late afternoon and she awoke rejuvenated. Adam was asleep and she slid down and took him in her mouth. He awoke and grew, as if dreaming of Popeye's spinach.

"There it is," she whispered and crawled atop and rode.

Adam moaned and his face scrunched in strange excruciating expressions.

"What? What?" Kaci asked, she'd stopped moving.

"Headache, but keep going, keep going," he said rubbing his forehead with his right hand, her clitoris with the thumb of his left.

Kaci bounced in an effort to bring about a quick finale, for him, hers could come another day. Twice was plenty already. It wasn't quick, but it happened eventually, for both. His splash caused a sensational stir, bringing about a wash of pleasure. She cried out and a door creaked closed behind them.

Adam moved his hand from his head and the nub was a full bulge. The skin had darkened from bright red to brown. Kaci screamed and rolled off Adam, instinctively clenching to hold in the sperm chowder trying to drip free.

She grabbed for a towel and held it beneath her raw and tenderized lips. "Adam, your head… the door, too," she gasped.

"Don't worry it was only the closet. It's an old house and we're bouncing around."

"Maybe we better take you to a—"

Adam folded his arms over his bare chest. "I'm not leaving until I talk to my parents. I have things to ask them, things I remember and don't understand." He fingered the bulge gently as he spoke. "I can't go until I understand."

Kaci didn't argue, as it was obviously important and perhaps there was expired penicillin in the cupboard to hold him over until they returned to the real world.

Dressed and medicated with a Claritin and three antibiotic pills from a blue container dated almost three years earlier, Adam stood over the stove stirring the small pot of chilli he'd found in the refrigerator. It smelled divine, different, but perfect.

It tasted as good as it smelled.

Adam finished most of his bowl and leaned back registering the meat. "I think this is squirrel or badger."

Kaci stopped and let that sink. She was hungry and it didn't matter, not right then.

"Did you often eat little animals?"

"No, only on special occasions, Christmas, Easter, the Shedding."

"The Shedding?"

"Snake thing, don't worry. I'm thinking we'd best call it a night early, what do you say?"

"I'm not so tired, but I have a book. You feeling all right?"

"I'm tired, that's all. We'll use the rooms my parents deigned for us. They don't need to know of the debauchery this afternoon. Imagine if they'd come home early and saw us. They'd never speak to me again."

"But they didn't. I can clean up. You go on up, whenever."

Adam finished and thanked her before retiring to bed with his suitcase. Kaci washed the dishes, went around straightening the sex bumped objects, fixed the sheets in the master bedroom, and finally visited the washroom before she went off to her plotted space in the sewing room with a book.

She checked her cellphone off and on, Twitter, Facebook, Instagram. Then she checked the clock and finally set aside a Gemma Files paperback and killed the lamp. Sleep came quickly and dipped into the topic of the day, prior to all the fucking. The old times and her mostly trustworthy memory.

Sweltering, everything wore sheen as if a mist hovered beyond sight. The moisture came from within, sucked out by the impossible heat. Trees, rocks, grass, and dirt, sweat poured forth, and Kaci watched from little girl eyes as a young woman stood before a young man and rubbed his face while chains held his arms and legs firm to a wooden post. The sun overhead pounded fire onto the red world until a shadow stepped in and offered a slight reprieve to Kaci.

"Don't think we can't smell it in you, devil," the woman seethed.

There was a comforting breeze that drew close at Kaci's side. Small hands wrapped small fingers around her small arm.

"Boy, don't you sense evil? All Eves balance on a pin, ready to fall for the easy stance on firm ground. When Satan whispered, what did he say?" the woman said as the boy clung to Kaci's side.

A massive black snake slithered on the red dirt between the woman's legs. Kaci stomped and growled. The boy let go, fearful of her rather than the snake.

Kaci's heartache rode so true and deep that it awoke her from the dream. Darkness cloaked the sewing room still, meaning she needed to attempt more sleep.

"Dreaming of a brother you don't have," she said instantly understanding the feeling of closeness lingering from her dream. The world had obviously mingled with her imagination to create a myth.

"Brother you do," a soft, slow voice said from the end of the room. "How did you find him? The devil, I reckon."

"Who's there?" Kaci pulled the covers tight to her chin.

The light switch flicked and showered the room with a yellow glow.

"Our Adam would never do what you did today, all over this home, 'less the devil came to play. We are the children of God and you've drove our son to malicious sin. Doubly sinful on such an important day."

There was a man at the end of the bed. He wore a white shirt with the buttons open to his hairy naval. The shirt was old and worn to translucent. He had grey hair and long thin scars criss-crossing his forehead and bald scalp.

He stood from the bench where he'd been and pointed a long black rifle. "Get up, devil."

Kaci shook her head in fear. The man yanked the blanket from her hands and any perception of safety offered by the cotton departed as she slid to the edge of the bed. She wore her pajamas: shorts and a t-shirt. The ancient t-shirt read *STOP GHOSTWOOD Save the Pine Weasel*.

Her feet found floor, but her legs were weak and shaky. She wondered if this man was Adam's father or some maniac that knew Adam. The realization struck that she and Adam had at least one person watching them since they'd arrived.

"Where's Adam?"

"He's with his mother, ready, the first shed is always the hardest, but I reckon if the good Lord sees fit, He'll forgive Adam what you made him do. If not, Adam will understand why we pick our fruit careful like. How did you find him?"

The entire time the man spoke, the rifle directed Kaci toward the door with twitchy wrist flicks. She moved as instructed.

"I didn't find him. I think you're maybe sick. Please, think this through, you're misunderstanding and overreacting. We're in love and—"

"How did you find him, devil?"

"What? We met in college, at a, at a bar, a coincidence," Kaci stammered, but that wasn't exactly right.

She'd set out, restless and looking for something after a telephone call from her father. It was a few minutes to midnight. She decided to walk to the café three blocks away for a bowl of ice cream. Before she got there, she found herself suddenly thirsty and intrigued by the sounds coming from within *Little Steady*. She stepped into the blues bar wearing the least flattering outfit she'd ever worn out of the dorm and ordered two beers. She didn't want two, but destiny overtook and she strode across the dance floor to a lonely man sitting at a table. He had tears in his eyes and an empty bottle in front of him.

Kaci sensed the words rather than thought them: *Maybe it's for the best she's gone.* Adam lifted his head and forced a weak smile. That was years earlier and they'd been together since. Such a strange chance meeting. Never before had she been so oddly bold, especially not sober and ready dressed for farmhand day labor.

"There is no such thing. There is one master and one trickster, everything happens for a reason. You know, I smell that trickster on you. I didn't for a long time, but Mother, she always smelled it and she always saw it. Down, move."

Doing as told, stepping down the stairs, she wanted to scream for Adam. She wanted the entire scene to be some poorly considered joke, a gag on the new girl in the family. Unfortunately, it didn't feel that way.

"I'd blast you back to Hell right now if it was possible. I'd burn you up, devil," the man said as the tips of the barrels stabbed into Kaci's back.

A dull pain shivered inside and she increased her speed. At the direction of the shotgun, Kaci moved toward the door where they'd first entered the home, where she'd lost the first article of clothing during the marathon of sensational decadence.

The heavy wooden door sat open a crack and she stepped outside into the night. From the side of the house, light, horribly red, came from within the barn. The cracks let the red spill in long ominous streams through the night. She didn't need another nudge. She knew where to go.

The grass was soft under her feet and the gravel was the polar opposite, hard and painful against her soles. From within the barn she heard a constant hiss and pushed through a tremendous heat.

"Go on then, just like last time when those unbelievers stole you and sided with Satan," the man said.

A scream bubbled from deep in her diaphragm. The man was nuts. Whatever he thought he knew wasn't fact. It was insane fantasy, a fanatic's wealth of craziness. Instead of screaming or fighting, she pulled open the wooden door and stared into the disarming light.

"Eve," a voice hissed from within.

That voice. It was a history lesson. It brought forth the dreams of the old times before her adoption. It carried all the memories she'd cast aside as fiction and all the memories her brain buried beneath rationality.

"Mother, you're *my* mother," she whispered. A push from behind moved her along.

Hisses bounded as the floor swayed and slithered away from her. Snakes circled and climbed onto the mother for protection.

"Look'it! They know you're evil!" shouted the man.

Adam was across the room. Kaci's heart flooded with different, battling emotions. The loudest of which was disgust. They'd shared so much, shared everything. They were of a split egg, Adam and Eve, the coming of serpent's reign. Sister and brother, twins, all of the wonderful wedding ideas sullied by putrid closeness.

Wrong love.

But oh how she loved him still and those emotions screamed seeing him chained to a post, the bulge in his forehead massive and blackened. Suddenly, she fully understood the ugliness of impossible and unfortunate attraction.

Wrong fucking love.

"Down, on your knees, devil," the man said and the shotgun's stock struck hard against the back of her leg.

Kaci fell and saw anxious serpents rush and turn tail as she made eye contact. They were skittish, but only of her. These were the holy relics of tradition long foregone in a modern world aching for civility.

"Oh Lord," the mother started, her voice raspy and booming, "You've called out to us and delivered our Adam to the true faith. He is of Your embodiment, written in Your image, please keep his will strong, and his power straight. Satan is sinister and relentless, our numbers are few, but with Adam comes a new home, just as the Christ, the second serpent son led our souls into the promised land. Here! The rebirth of Your first serpent son, the rebirth of Adam's true self can close the gates and block the dark man's entry!

"Shed! Shed, son of the serpent in the sky, shed!"

"Adam?" Kaci attempted to rise.

Adam shook and struggled within his flesh.

The barrel stock struck into the center of Kaci's back and she fell, wincing. Snakes of all sizes and shapes slithered and hissed. They grew frantic with the theriomorphic display of Adam's evolution. His head and scalp bulged further and the heat in the room intensified as if burning away anything impure or unwanted. Thick, heavy sweat clung to Kaci like slime.

Adam screamed and his voice choked away into a hiss as his skull split and a fat brown serpent's face burst forth. The chained body slumped like an empty snowsuit.

"Let the Lord lead you!" shouted the mother.

The weapon wielding man cheered in agreement. From the floor, Kaci eyed the slithering monster's approach. It was incredible and massive. It hissed, revealing dripping yellowy fangs and an unhealthy interest.

"Adam," Kaci moaned and closed her eyes, awaiting pain and demise. The heavy slither drew closer. A hiss rang louder than the chorus of miniature voice boxes surrounding her. King of the serpents. Vibrations traveled through the floor. Kaci shook with fear.

"Adam, please," she sobbed and opened her eyes to the heat of an unhinged jaw and a sharp, knife-like tongue stabbing at her face.

That quick movement sprang a rapid, thoughtless voice she knew belonged to someone else, the same voice that had offered a drink in a blues bar years ago.

"Adam, think of the things I'll do. Think of the pleasure. Think of our love. This is not natural. The nature of man is not serpent, you've fallen from logic, and you need to take it back. I can help you."

The tongue slashed again and fangs sunk as the incredible jaw came down over Kaci. The bite pierced her shoulders and dragged her home several inches.

The voice bubbled despite her urge to cry out. "You

do this and we both die. Taste me, Adam. I taste wrong because you are not right. You are not a serpent. You are a mammal, a man, my love, my brother. Stop this madness, Adam."

The fangs retracted a half-inch.

"You love me and I love you. Woman and man."

The fangs retracted further and the mouth reeled in reverse. Kaci slid loose as Adam slithered away, fighting an internal demon.

"Devil!" the man said.

Adam shot upwards in a crooked arch. Reptilian attack rainbow. A heavy mannish cry rode above the hissing. The man, the vessel father, dropped his rifle with a clank.

Kaci turned her eyes to Adam devouring the man, his fat slimy jaw rode over the flesh and bone, and that flesh and bone thrashed from within while acids broke the man down, forcing poison into the lungs searching for oxygen.

"Adam, this is Satan! The work of the Lord is hard and long! You must stop and heed the message!" the mother shouted.

Kaci existed as a sidekick within her body. Something lifted her. A smile stretched. She howled with laughter. The figure inside Adam's maw ceased its fight and Adam coiled sleepily.

"Eve, evil," the mother said. "Children!"

The fearful snakes rushed forward and snapped their jaws, tiny poisonous fangs clamping onto Kaci as she rose from her knees. Snakes had attached and clung to every inch of flesh. She wore them like tassels as she approached the mother in a slow, but steady amble.

"Devil! Devil! Adam, please!" the mother shouted.

Adam was sluggish as she turned to face the scene. The snakes latching and then falling away dead from the venomous sweat coating Kaci like caramel on

Halloween apples. More snakes leapt and clung only to eventually fall. Her laughter flowed into a heinous cackling, filling the barn as the hissing died away one creature at a time.

Confused, Adam forced his body forward. The weight of his father was a tremendous burden to digest and transport. Adam watched, helpless. Kaci leaned down over their frightened mother. The old woman looked pathetic in her ceremonial sandals made from an old python friend, and neck to thigh denim, vest and shorts; ratty off-white tee beneath.

Kaci bent further, knees to the floor, and kissed their mother with fiery breath. The final, wilful snakes fell away, dead.

Beneath Kaci, the vessel mother stiffened. Shook. Crumbled into dust.

Kaci rose straight and peered onto the fat ten-foot snake wearing the eyes of a man named Adam. She smiled at him, almost apologetically. The instinct and the voice that brought them together fuelled her motion and words, but deep down she bore burning love and pity.

Adam focussed past Kaci and to his mother, knowing now that he'd made a mistake. She was an ash pile awaiting a strong breeze to blow her into a million fragmented memories.

"Adam, poor Adam. I will never forget what we had," Kaci said and reached down to pull his heavy snake face to hers. His tongue jutted and rode against her tongue.

A great river of fire swelled within Adam, hardening his veins. Erasing him.

Kaci dropped her fiancé, nothing more than a dusty mound, and stepped out of the barn.

~

For all of the hours driving and flying she thought of

the trick her father showed her as a small girl. As she practiced then, it became obvious that she'd used it many times before and would use it again in the future.

Take a memory you don't like, think of it five times a day, but in a favorable way. Do that for a week and the bad memory isn't so bad, you might even turn it into a good memory. Eventually, it will never bother you again.

She'd do that concerning Adam and everything else in the barn, but not until she spoke to her father. There was something she recalled on the night the excommunicated snake-handlers rescued her from death and became her faux-parents, took her on a long trip north.

Into the home. Her father was single again so there was no worry of startling some poor girlfriend with the sight of hundreds of fang marks all over her face. She'd worn a great deal of cover-up, but people stared when she passed through customs, sat beneath a scarf on the plane, and stopped for food on the road. She didn't blame them.

"Dad?" she called out.

"In the den, Kaci." He wore a smile on his voice.

Kaci stepped through the familiar home and into the den. Her father had a book on parasitic love stories in his lap. His smile faded as he drank in the image of his faux-daughter.

"So Adam was *that* Adam?"

She spied him, equal parts furious and curious. "You knew?"

"Not really, but I wondered if it would come. You can never know about these things."

"But why, and…" Tears fell.

"Don't cry honey, it's over now, yeah?"

She nodded.

"You remember the trick?"

She nodded again.

"Good. You hungry?"

She shook her head and turned away, she made it to the kitchen before she heard his voice again.

"Praise Satan!" he called out.

"Praise Satan," she whispered.

The Weight of Solitude, the Pressure of Conscience

Lee Henry sat behind the wheel of his gold, 1988 Ford Tempo tapping his finger against the outside panel of the driver's door. The light hanging overhead was red. The song on the radio was a new tune from Hammer and it really thumped, not that his speakers did it any justice.

The light turned green as Hammer's jam faded into something else. A flavor of the month R&B girl band began a slow moan and Lee flipped the AM/FM switch. It was a pain to find the station once you'd left it. It was better to wait out the whining with talk radio than to scroll around the abyss of radio land. Though talk radio was far from free of whining.

Two men discussed the universe and the busy business of drumming up attention for NASA in a time after moonwalking and the space race. The public had lost interest and that meant funding was apt to dry-up.

Through the rain damp streets, Lee made his way to

the highway southbound while the men spoke of the good old days. It made Lee think of his grandfather, a smiling man who always wore blue suspenders and had eyebrows so bushy they seemed poised to leap from his face. Lee didn't have much contact with his grandfather in the normal way. The man was always on the move. Lee's parents scoffed at this, as if a man of that age ought to have come to some settlement with life, drop anchor and hunker down until the cold winter took him.

That was not what Lee saw. The man had it right, even as a small boy Lee knew that. He fantasized about journeying the world, seeing all the crazy things people of all their different shades got up to. In a small way, he was right there with him by standing against the norm and offering a silent thumbs up to the man's itchy feet.

It didn't happen as often as the boy would've liked, but once every few weeks, times linked and the winds blew. The speaker on the ancient Grundig *shh-chuched* and his grandfather said, "Lee, you there boy?"

The Grundig was a forty-pound magic shoebox of steel and glass tubes. It wasn't only Lee's grandfather out there on the airwaves. There were all kinds of people, from all over the world. There were also those strange pattern stations, blipping in repetition, old wartime conversation forever pinging the airwaves with voice.

Lee often imagined stumbling upon the spot where that forgotten radio sent out its signals. What he'd do when he got there, that was never really part of it. Discovery was enough. He didn't even need to plant a flag like the Americans did on the moon.

The topic on the radio shifted and brought Lee from reverie.

It was a month into spring. From the corner of his eye, Lee saw his first fawn of the season. The mother was nowhere in sight, but that was how it happened sometimes.

He drove past the darting animal and onto the ramp out of the city.

~

Tennessee Smith rolled a full minivan. The grandchildren sang and the wife sang. He'd tried to push the classics, but nothing beat the New Kids. It had been a good day up in the city. They'd gone shopping at the liquidation outlet, visited the Toys R' Us, and stopped by the pier. Only one hundred feet out, they saw a pair of shooting splashes from a humpback pod. Pretty cool.

"Okay, sit down. Don't need a ticket, do we?" the old man said, question posed, but all understood the rhetorical nature.

A gold Tempo passed on his right moments before orange cones shrank the three-lane highway to two lanes. Instinctively, his foot lifted and the Aerostar slowed. In the back, the middle boy of the seven children cupped hands around his mouth and then shouted, "Cartoon Indians!"

The old man smiled and played along, tapping his hand over a yawning set of lips as he said *awwww.* TV had a way of getting everything screwy. At least the kids knew the difference between themselves and the feather and loincloth *redskins* on Bugs Bunny. The visual differences probably made it easy enough, really, the only similarities between them and the images were feathers (though only at ceremonies) and black hair.

To the left of the Aerostar, a tanker truck barrelled a couple clicks faster than the Smiths rolled. The TV Indian sounds ceased and for a breath, the only noise was the low radio and the wheeze of the cracked driver's window. Hearing the hissing air reminded Tennessee that there was no time like the present to light a cigarette. He lifted his pack from his breast pocket and slipped a stick between his lips.

Netty held out her hand for the pack. The sound from the back perked up again. Tennessee used the dash lighter to ignite his smoke. As he lifted his eyes from the tip of the cigarette, a red Mazda Miata fired by, sneaking between the truck and the minivan. The truck blared its horn and Netty jumped in her seat.

The children howled laugher, making honking noises.

Tennessee smiled his final old man smile. He had six real teeth left on the bottom and nine on the top. He figured a few more ought to do it before he had them yanked and replaced with a Fixodent ready set of falsies.

Ahead, the gold Tempo switched lanes, nearly driving the Miata into the pylons. The Mazda broke hard and swung its wheels, skidding black streaks and loud rubbery squeals. The truck driver did not think through his actions and fought against the immediate trouble of crushing the Mazda.

The nose of the truck plowed into the rear of the Aerostar, sending it sideways. It tipped. The truck bounced, the heavy tank payload caught up and passed. The hot tar within sloshed, aching for freedom. Three vehicles smashed into the tanker in short order.

The children had begun screaming. Tennessee hoped they'd be okay.

The scent of hot filth filled the air and he expected otherwise. The fire on the hood sprouted and the oozing stink chased forward. Everywhere were sounds of pain and terror.

Tennessee stared out his window at the gold Tempo as it pulled into the cordoned-off right lane, safe and fine.

~

Lee Henry pleaded his case. There was a bear cub on the highway and that's why he switched lanes. Besides, the Mazda was speeding. The court found him not guilty while his ever-ringing telephone suggested the court of public opinion deemed him a monstrous criminal.

The cries of pain were everywhere. He heard it when he slept. He heard it when he attempted sleep. He heard it in the voices of his accusers. He heard it from the beaks of birds. The clanging and crunching metal. The screams. Human voices expressed a terror beyond imagination.

I'm burning!

It was hot carnage.

The driver of the overturned transport wrestled within his cab, screaming as he attempted to climb out his door window while bubbling tar spilled over him, cooking him, peeling him, consuming him in the excruciating liquid wave.

Help me!

There were other voices.

Save me, please!

Help! It burns! Help me!

Lee bore this memory, the only survivor witnessing the front end. Others saw it, but from behind. They had stopped in time so that they didn't become part of Lee's kill-count.

Twelve died under the flaming tar.

The message on the answering machine tape featured a world of hurt. A woman explained the loss of her parents and children. Told stories of each member connected along living lines, humanizing them so Lee understood what he'd done. And he listened. It was penance.

"Hello, you've reached Henry Lee, leave a message."

"What you did to my family is unforgivable, my people never forget. We are small in life, but strong and big in death. You better pray what the elders say ain't true. Better pray all the old magic is only on TV," the raspy feminine voice with a slow drawl said before she hung up with a loud slam. An hour later, she would call back. "My youngest was Mary, she was six and could braid and liked to read stories. She liked cartoons. Children like cartoons when they aren't dead."

The telephone was incessant.

Lee covered his head, never wanting to converse, but needing to hear.

"Lee, are you there? I know what happened. It's me, it's Michelle."

This was unexpected and still he didn't move. The message was short, that evening Michelle called again. This time he rushed to his telephone and scooped up the receiver. Michelle was a friend and ex-girlfriend. She was a link to the old Lee who hadn't killed with his reaction to a bear cub.

"Michelle?" he whispered.

"I heard. I heard and I'm so sorry," she said and he spilled. All the pain and terror, the hopeless state and the impossible future. She waited and listened. "I have a friend and he has an idea and a connection to a job up north."

The remote posting was a chance for a new start. The further north one moves, the more jobs they immediately become qualified to operate. Fit based on willingness rather than experience, and still, he knew a little something about radios and transmissions. He knew more than enough to learn on the job.

In late September, Lee began his new life at the small weather research station at Tip North on Ellesmere Island in Canada's arctic, approximately 4,100 miles directly north of Green Bay, Wisconsin, U.S.A. The air was fresh and crisp. He'd never smelled such nothingness. The wind whistled. He still heard the screams, but with time and space, maybe…

The daylight hours were long yet, though getting shorter, quickly.

The downtime outweighed the tasks by a vast margin.

There was equipment designed for the climate. Lee monitored everything, righted any wrongs, brushed away blown ice particles, and kept watch that the wildlife did nothing to harm the government's property.

It was odd and cleansing. There was a world outside the world and if not for the voices on the radio and the face on the scratchy, fuzzy satellite uplink, he was alone in a way that most human beings never experience. The face in his coffee joked that he was another of the bears.

The smile was forced and flat. Joking was a stretch yet.

There were two rooms in the station. One housed his sleeping, bathing, and eating quarters and the other room had a large computer, the radios, the television, the VCR, and the stacks of books and video cassettes.

Five months cut off. The seclusion *had* to be the perfect medicine. There was nothing else. Routine helped. He worked and slept, had short conversations on the enormous radio. He didn't like the satellite uplink. It was intrusive. The singularity was a blanket and he swaddled.

The remembered voices lessened daily.

Books, movies, and music became his only contact with the *real* world outside the airwaves. These were controlled samples. The big radio connected him to the Eureka station far to the south. Eureka remained well within the realm of the arctic, long from the real world.

Using the big radio brought home the past, the forever calling numbers stations and the BBC music that never went away. It was as if he rebooted to before. This was good. This was necessary.

The winds had ceased screaming in agony and instead only screamed their motion.

When he tried to punish himself for moving forward, the din of highway chaos refused him. Part of his being clung to the need for punishment, like a drunk finding new apologies to dole before reaching the next step.

On agitated days, when the permafrost glaze riding over the surface danced and removed vision beyond a few feet, Lee actually sought salvation from the big radio system. The white walls around the station pounded home the feelings of singularity and isolation in all the wrong ways. So much so that that Lee turned the dials and listened for *anything*.

He assumed this was part of the process of healing.

"As if you're one needing healed."

Talking to himself was normal, utterly normal.

On the radio, the silence was nearly complete, only the whistle of the fence around the small compound and the fans built into his equipment blew audible pollution into his ears. The ghostly spy calls from wartimes did nothing for him and he spun in search of living, breathing life.

The storm whipped the white mid-November into frenzy. Lee stared into the whitewash, his gaze reaching no more than a few feet beyond the port window. It was the first real winter storm to remove vision from the limited daylight. By then he'd come to crave the shortening periods of sunshine. The rays were a comrade to lose in the vastness of that white abyss.

Right then, coffee cup in hand, gawking into the whipping white, he'd never felt so claustrophobic and lonely. For a tick of the clock, he considered donning his thermal gear and stepping out, if only to step out, widen the walls around him.

Instead, there was a crackle from the speaker.

Lee stepped to his radio and said, "Tip North, hello?"

There was fuzz and static.

"Anyone out there, come back?" a gruff mannish voice asked.

Lee jumped. His insides melted with something like gratitude. He pulled the steel microphone with the heavy square base to his lips and said, "Hello?"

"Oh geez, I finally found somebody. How's it going?"

A thousand questions streamed into Lee's mind. "Fine, who is this?"

"I'm Percy. So what's it like where you are. It's stormy as hell here. I used to go all over, but I've never seen weather like this. Ever take a real vacation, like on a beach I mean?"

"No. I went to Japan once. I don't remember much. It was muggy. My name is Lee Henry, by the way."

"Japan, makes sense, you got one of those names, but I guess Lee usually comes at the end. Or is that a coincidence. I'm a bit of a hick when it comes to that stuff."

"Uh, no, I think that's right, only surnames and I don't know if it's Japanese that have Lee…"

"Hey, no worries. It's all Chinese to me. So where— You know what? No. Look, I've got a long stay and I don't want to wear out conversation. I'll call out to you later. I got your station now. You better write down mine. How did you find me?"

Lee looked at the radio as if for the first time. The dial was not where he left it in case of emergency contact. "I, uh, I thought you found me."

"Ha, crazy. Talk to you later."

Outside, the wind whistled and Lee felt truly okay for the first time in several months. The accident was as far away in mind as it was in reality. The sensation did not last and Lee fell into longing within a week. The days grew shorter and the nights ate the world. The mounting aloneness and abandonment of humanity wore him thinner.

Through November, he wondered if he'd made a mistake, or if someone played a trick on him. *Percy*. He longed for contact and that was absurd.

~

December first, he'd finished his morning duties and the sun had nearly set. Outside the small fenced compound, two bears wrestled in the final glimpses of gold. He watched the bears and sometimes they watched him.

"Lee, Tip North, Lee, come in."

"Tip North, I'm here," Lee said, relieved that contact came, but annoyed that it was not the contact he wanted.

"How are the Eskimo wanderers, see any lately? Did you take a peek at the link-ups for the video yet? It says it's receiving, but it's black."

It was Bradley Terrier, the Francophone accent was a giveaway. Terrier came from Northern New Brunswick, used to hard conditions and radio communication. He considered regular chatter necessary, audio and visual. He was also an asshole with a decidedly unfunny way about him. Having Bradley as his only regular contact was not an easy task.

Lee had placed a piece of foil tape over the camera lens and left his monitor powered down. On their second video call—choppy and fuzzy as it was—Terrier thought it funny to bend over with his ass out.

"No, I don't see the problem. I'm not too worried."

"I thought you were 'sposed to be good with the electronics. Hell, I figured you'd tune around the shortwave. You do any of that? On clear nights, I bet you can find folks in the real world," Terrier said.

Lee wasn't in the mood to discuss the others on the radio. Besides, on clear nights he found only numbers stations and music. It was during a storm that he met the mysterious Percy.

"Not really," he said.

"Well I gots to big Pow-Wow with Ottawa here, so I better jet…"

Static overtook Terrier's voice and then, "Help-shh-shit-shh-shh-me!'"

Lee's heart jumped at the high, tormented voice.

"… Hey, big shitty boy," Terrier's voice came back.

Lee said, "Did you hear that? There was a woman."

"Interference? That happens sometimes, usually a radio play of some sort. It's crazy, radio signals keep going on forever."

Lee leaned back from his desk and stepped to one of the porthole windows. There was a fence and there was winter, permanent winter. Days of silence.

Lee had begun to wonder if he hadn't imagined Percy.

~

"Hey, Mr. Henry! What's happening?"

Lee broke from the window, outside the weather was up to winter business and the moon was gone. Overhead greens and blues dashed and swayed. He picked up the microphone. So little happened, Lee answered truthfully without thought. "Hi. The bears fight a lot. It's pretty neat to see them."

"Neat! Ten-four, good buddy. We got them here too, fighting like crazy. I remember when I was a kid, we had bears come and get into our trash all the time. Those bears are nothing on these guys, holy crow! I've never seen so many bears as I do in the north. Neat is the word for it."

"Where are—?" Lee began, cut off.

"Oh dang, sorry buddy. Talk to you later."

The communication died.

~

Lee straightened overturned radars and meters, cleared away ice and snow, and watched the bears watch him. He wore a black parka, a balaclava beneath the heavy parka hood, thermal pants, and thermal boots. It was thirty-seven below centigrade and the sun shined somewhere, but no longer onto Tip North.

Surely the sun hadn't died.

Stationed near a coast, the animal activity was busy. Big and intimidating. Bears sat beyond the fence, their eyes glinting in the gloom, now and then catching the yard light glow.

Days mounted. Terrier was regular and annoying. Percy was allusive and mysterious.

"What?" Lee asked, coming back from pondering Percy.

"I was saying, it's important to keep in contact, hold the reins. You know what I mean? The mind can play some freaky games when you're alone out here."

"Right, I was—there was a bear rattling a fence outside," he said trying to explain away any missed conversation.

"Better hope Nanook isn't out there too." Terrier laughed his high asshole laugh.

"Nanook?"

"God and master of the polar bears. If Nanook decides to, he'll send the troops for you. Some think he's good, but many know the truth. Dun-dun-duh." He laughed higher, louder. "I had a grandma that chummed with some Inuits, they had old stories about all the animal gods and how the greatest gods watched over all the tribes and souls in the sky. Not all the tribes knew about the Great Bear God in life, but Nanook knew them and watched over all those living *of* the earth. I don't believe none of that shit, don't let my ponytail fool ya!"

Lee huffed. "Right, well. I'll talk to you later. I think I might take a siesta."

"Good idea. Keep cool, Mr. Big Shitty."

It was such an odd thing to focus on, being from a city. Then again, any difference will do when sticking a name.

"Keep cool… you shithead."

Keeping cool was not an issue, nor were polar bear

gods. He lay down, a Slick Rick cassette rolling to assist drowning any thoughts that might keep him from his nap. It hadn't been much of a problem lately. He'd never been so tired.

Lee awoke to darkness around him and a scratching sound outside the door. He rose and stumbled for a light he didn't recall switching off. Through the porthole window was the darkness and the long shadows cast by the yard lamp. Overhead, bright greens and purples waged war across the sky.

The scratching was loud and it had nothing to do with the Northern Lights. Lee stepped across the room and to another porthole window. Snow had blown over the glass and he tapped to knock it free. Three knocks after an initial tap shifted the white blanket. Lee gasped. Out in the vast forever night, through a tiny gap in the snow cover, a humanistic silhouette stood beyond the fence in the big moon's shine.

"How the hell?"

The silhouette turned, blueish eyes flashed amid the gloom.

"Dear Go—"

A giant paw slammed against the glass and Lee fell to the cold floor. The paw came down again. The sound was drum heavy. Lee crab-slid backwards a full body length. Adrenaline stiffened his muscles.

Minutes passed and Lee crept to the window and peered out. The moon was high behind thin cloud cover. The barren landscape was void of life. The image before him shifted further into normalcy.

At noon, the quality of the black had changed and the dim cast of southern sun travelled to Tip North. "How long—?" Lee began to ask when the radio crackled and Terrier's voice carried.

"Are you there? Lee, Tip North, are you there?"

Lee raced to the microphone and yanked it up by the

base.

"I'm here, I'm here."

"You didn't log last night's readings."

"Huh?

"The readings."

Damn. Shirking duty was unprofessional and not in character. Right then, Lee nearly vocalized an incredible and incredibly stupid notion that the mythical bear god was at fault. He managed to reel back the insane notion before it became words. "I did them, guess I had a glitch or I didn't hit save or something." His voice was hoarse.

"No worries, one missed night isn't going to change much. How're the bears?"

"Bears? No trouble with bears."

"I should hope not, you so much as break a leg out there and you're a goner…"

"Shh-me!-shh-shh-burning!" a voice floated in.

Lee's breath caught in his throat. He knew that voice and he'd gone north to erase it. It wasn't how it had been. When the guilt feasted, he'd always understood sounds coming from within rather than those from without.

This was a voice in the world.

Terrier came back on a wave of shouting voices and radio hisses. "… better. Over and out…"

"Oh, okay."

"Shh-shh-my daughter-shh-shh-burning!"

"You're breaking up," Lee said knowing well that it wasn't that. If he could fool himself then maybe he'd be all right.

"Jesus, man, I said, Eureka out."

"No, but, I heard," he muttered, microphone at an arm's length.

~

Lee fiddled with the dials searching for the voices. Nothing, back and forth, nothing. He straightened his spine. The clock on the corner of the computer monitor suggested several hours had disappeared.

"Damn, damn." He took the readings from each of the monitors. He was late and a day after he'd missed reports altogether. "They fire you and then where will you be? Back in Vancouver, back…" he didn't say it.

Back in a world that hungered for his blood.

"Shh-shh-back from-shh," the radio squawked.

Shaken, he yanked the volume dial to zero. Outside, the scratching had returned. Shocked and terrified, Lee rose and then fell, crumpled under the weight of his body. He cried out and bore a fantastic hunger and thirst. There was no explanation.

Above, the volume rose and fell, swooping voices in and out. Fragments of angry callers, burned victims, Bradley Terrier, and then settling a moment for Percy.

"Hey, buddy, Mr. Henry. Just checking in. It's a cold one, gets the bears a movin'! Talk to you later."

The radio ceased and Lee crawled toward the kitchenette in his living space. The door that led into the frozen forever quivered and bulged inwards like tin siding facing off with a thrown baseball. The scratching gouged at the steel like a junkyard crusher, growing faster and *thicker* by the second before becoming a thrumming, thumping vibration. The door had a paddle release on the inside. A pin dangled by a chain. There had never been a reason to lock it before.

"Not happening," Lee whispered as he slid to the fridge.

Above him, the windowed door bulged and shook. The fridge mimicked. He closed his eyes and bet on the most logical situation. It wasn't an intruder. It was hunger and thirst. He'd almost killed himself with fatigue, losing time sitting at the radio trying to escape the loneliness around him.

Blindly, he swung open the fridge and dug for

sustenance. Obtained, chewed, downed. Replenished, Lee leaned away from everything that had moved, despite it's naturally stilled status, remaining on the floor.

~

"Nanook, you're not real. There are no Arctic gods," he said as he rinsed silverware. It felt good to say. Lee imagined somehow chartering a helicopter and flying down to Eureka Station to punch Terrier for putting the idea in his head. "Nanook, you're a fraud. I am the master of the north, not you!" Lee donned a goofy grin. "Nanook, you're a bit—"

The scratching at the far side of door returned. Words failed the only man on the planet at that lattitude. He slunk away from the sink and dropped into the chair at the small dining table.

The radios sat silent, the wind howled but far into the distance, the scratching had ceased, and again there was nothing so pure and thick it was as if his ears ceased collection.

Through the night and into the morning, nothing.

Without the voices stealing time, he counted each second twice. The loneliness was everything. No other choice, he put his face down and focussed.

Vigilant, Lee worked, two days in a row without issue.

Evening, December eighth, outside was a palm blue plane where the yard light touched and a black beyond. High up, the sky danced a green display. Lee was okay and the world was good, the world was…

Long and loud, the steel on the outside of the building creaked as if torn at by the claws of an abominable snowman. A screech erupted from within and he forewent any promise of logic and sensibility. As he would when he was a small boy who slept under glow-in-the-dark stars on the ceiling while tuning into his Grundig, Lee rushed across the room and slid under his bed covers and the sleeping bag.

The station lights flickered and sputtered before dowsing as if sucked dry. "Not happening," he said and further buried himself in the warm cocoon. "Cabin fever. It's all in your head. Think about it, Lee."

Time shifted and he laughed at himself. Fear was stupid. There was no pounding. And if there was, hiding under a cotton wall did nothing to prevent it. Stupid. Childish.

He poked from his sleeping bag, above him, the neon stars brought home safe familiarity and comfort. It was a good place, at home in bed, his parents just down the hall… *Wait.* He exhaled a long held breath and watched a cloud puff out from his lips.

Green light danced the sky's ballroom floor. His body cried out in surprise and numb ache at the sudden cold. This was all wrong.

"No! Not happening!" He leapt to his feet. Flaming pins stabbed into his frozen toes as he ran the dozen steps to the station door. The handle shook under his grip. It wouldn't open. Frozen. Lee tugged and wailed, tears iced his cheeks while the moisture in his lungs crystalized. "Please, please." His moans wore a shimmy. Behind, a polar bear roared, charging toward him, gaining all too quickly. "Please." He pulled back with a great tug, the door swung outward and the confused man dove, clipping his toe on the frame.

Over his shoulder, bears remained beyond the fence. The memory screamed defiantly, *one slammed a window, they scratch at the door and you know it. There's one inside the fence!*

Sleeping bag yanked within, the door wheezed closed. Warmth stung his thawing body. He fell into a puddle.

He squeezed his knees tight to his chest and shook,

rubbing his feet. His toe ached long after the rest of him had warmed.

It was ten according to the clock. Lee needed a friend. He called out to Eureka on the radio and heard only static. Sniffing and damp, he spun the dial to where Percy existed. More static.

"Damn you." He returned the dial to the station's common frequency. Terrier's voice boomed over the tiny space. The volume jacked to jarring.

"...ee!"

"Ah!" Lee screeched in alarm.

"There you... stormy here... gain later ou..." Terrier said.

Heart thumping like a war drum, Lee glanced to the door and back to the large radio face before him.

~

He limped for a week, keeping his movements to a minimum. No storms took him outside to fix damaged equipment. Clear weather kept Percy away as well.

December twentieth, Lee ate oatmeal in a plastic dish.

"Shh-I'm burning! Help me! Shh-shh-shh-where you come-shh!"

"No!" Lee dropped his bowl. He stomped across the room, pain roaring from his sore toe, and turned the volume down on the radio. It had climbed to maximum once again, *somehow.*

"You're losing it, Lee Henry. Get it togeth..."

The radio barked. "Shh-unforgivable. Shh-we-shh-are-shh-shh-life, but strong-shh-shh-shh-death."

"Not happening."

Fresh air got no fresher than the Arctic. He dressed to escape the radio and his imagination. Minus forty, not counting the wind chill. The weather bit through the layers. Lee walked the perimeter. There were no bears beyond the fence, not that he saw—easing the grey matter pressure. Circles had a calming effect. For hours Lee stomped over the icy surface until sweat began to trickle. The warm drip broke him from his reverie. He gawked through the fence at thirty-four polar bears. One bear approached and then leaned up against the fence. Another followed. Lee stumbled away, his heavy boots slipping on the glassy permafrost floor.

More bears leaned on the chain links. It bowed.

Beyond the yard light, the Aurora Borealis made art of the cosmos, abstract until it wasn't. Not as one likens the clouds to shapes, but solid and certain, the greens, pinks, purples, and blues formed a bear's head.

The beast in the sky growled silently.

The leaning bears cried to their master.

"Not happening," Lee said as he forced his eyes away. The fence creaked and the bears growled again. "You're calling to Eureka and getting out."

He reached for the door and utter silence enveloped the universe as if pulled into a cosmic vacuum. Reason battled within. *Conquer your hallucination. It's simple. Just do it.* There were no bears on the fence, none in the sky. Lee turned to prove his stance against the faults of his mind.

"Not real!" he screamed at the crowded forms that stood only a few feet away.

Belief mattered none. The bears roared, many upright on hind legs, paws with claws reaching for man meat. Their breaths were a thick and fish stinking fog. Lee jumped, stunned.

"Go away, go," he mumbled as if shooing a cat. He turned to step around the steel as the latch let. A heavy paw came down on his back and sent his face into the door, slamming it shut. "No please, you can't be." He sobbed.

The pain in his face was incredible, strengthened by the cold. The bears roared around him and he curled into a ball. Ice crystals melted on his cheek. Permafrost burned at his exposed hands. The bears had gone quiet.

Frozen tears created clear humps beneath and beside Lee's eyes, drifting toward his ear. The bears were gone. The fence stood as it always had.

Exhausted and sweaty and yet cold, Lee crawled into bed after making his way inside, closing and locking the door behind him.

There was clarity when Lee awoke. His pillow was wet with thawed terror. Bradley Terrier had done this to him. The man planted the seed and needled him with fake radio communications.

He knows about the accident.

Lee radioed out to Eureka, but got no answer. It happened sometimes. He loaded a cassette into the stereo and went to the kitchen. After a short meal, he returned to the radio, he'd hand out a mighty verbal thrashing.

"Eureka Station, come back," he said and then for the first time, Lee heard himself bark aloud. "It was an accident!"

"Uh, Eureka here, what's an accident? Am I doing this right? Can you hear me?" The accent was minimal, not a trace of French.

"I hear you. Where's Terrier?"

There was an audible wheeze through the microphone. "Brad's gone."

"Gone?"

"Brad's gone, we were collecting samples a week ago and," there was a click and a pause, "a bear attacked us. We shot the bear, but it got Brad in a bad way. The thing came out of nowhere."

Lee gulped back an irrational bubble. "Is he…? A week ago?"

"Yeah, a week ago. He's still under I guess, they'll keep him that way until," as the man spoke, Lee roved his mouse and awoke the computer, "they bring him home from, well, from death."

The calendar on the toolbar stated December twenty-seventh. "Impossible."

"Yeah, but while I have you, I can't find your reports. I figured you and Brad had some other file set-up or something. Oh and Merry Christmas, if you're that type."

"How many days?" Lee gasped, not asking about the reports, but over the number of days since he'd crawled into bed afraid of shadows he'd surely imagined.

"A bunch anyway. Umm, if you resubmit the last eight or nine days that will do. Maybe to another inbox somewhere we have access."

"I can have those out by tonight, I suppose."

"You mean tomorrow night?"

Lee roved the mouse back over the clock and calendar. First thing, he rose and radioed Eureka Station. *First thing!* The clock read twenty-one twenty-two. It was only minutes after eleven the first time he radioed. When he finally got through it was no later than lunch.

"I don't… yeah, okay."

"Talk to you later, Tip North."

Lee put his head on his arms and closed his eyes as he leaned forward on the desk.

The radio screeched and hissed. "Shh-strong and big-shh-death. Shh-shh-shh."

The door quaked and rattled.

Steel screamed as cold claws tore through its brittle surface. Lee shook his head on his arms, the scent coming from his armpits was enough to make his eyes water.

"Shh-unforgiveable, do you hear me, Mr. Lee?" Piercy's voice rose higher and higher until squealing. "Small in life! Shh-strong and big in death. Shh-shh."

"Not happening!"

"Lee, you…!"

He lifted his head. That voice was familiar.

Steel screeched and freezing wind filled the room, stealing his attention. Lee looked away. He was hungry again, that's all. The kitchen was full of food and it was only steps away. He'd missed meals and slept too much and it…

"You can't wish us away, buddy." Percy's voice had returned to normal.

"Food, you need to eat," Lee said.

He opened the familiar cupboards, blindly tapping for a nutrient rich chocolate meal replacement. With greedy swallows, Lee finished one packet and grabbed for another. He closed his eyes and nothing had changed when he again gazed at his all too familiar quarters.

With a third protein pack, the filthy, odorous man stumbled toward his computer. His toe oozed a green pearl. The spreadsheet figures jumbled and ran. He put his head down again.

The radio crackled.

"Hello?"

Lee rolled his shoulders, his back ached terribly, slobber dangled from his sticky lips. He stared at the radio trying to comprehend the voice.

"Hello."

He picked up the microphone.

"Michelle?"

"Lee! Are you okay?"

"I wanna go home." He sobbed. "Please tell them to take me home."

"It's not a good time. People know you're a murderer, even if the courts decided you weren't. You can't come back, not now."

"Please, Michelle."

"Sorry, buddy."

"What?" Lee turned up the volume. "Michelle, come

back! Where… come on!" He fiddled with dials and knobs. Lee leaned back on his chair and wailed to the ceiling.

"Lee, you there, boy?"

He shook his head. His dead grandfather was even less likely than his ex-girlfriend. He'd lost it. There was no choice. He had to leave, be anywhere else. Eureka Station, he had to call and have them send help. Lee picked up the microphone.

The cord broke a foot prematurely.

"Who…? How…?" he rambled as he gawked at the frayed tendrils of ruined cord.

A high-pitched voice came through the speakers, increasing in volume. "Strong in death! Nanook controls all! Nanook is the master of all!"

The voices echoed the sentiment like a barbershop quartet. Crunching metal and flaming wreckage sounds filled in the background. A memorized and plaguing cacophony.

"Not happening," Lee whined defiantly into the crook of his elbow.

"You're gonna burn, cunt!"

"You killed my…"

"You'll die how they…"

"It's all your fault…"

"It was an accident!" Lee screamed and yanked the sixty-tree-pound radio receiver from his desk. "An accident!" He lifted the box over his head to smash it on the floor. It landed with a crackle-thump.

From the speaker came a steady hiss.

With the accident din chorus faded, the bears began growling, tinny on the airwaves. Full and rich beyond the door.

"No you're…!" Lee grabbed at his computer monitor and launched it across the room next. The voices continued to sing their taunts.

"It was an accident! A mistake!"

The ruined radio, the ruined monitor were quiet. Lee scanned the room for the source.

"There's nothing el—!" His chest pounded and his legs weakened. "Not possible!" On the shelf next to the door was the answering machine he'd left in Vancouver, cord dangling, unplugged, tiny speaker blaring at stadium crowd decibels.

"*Nanook is the god of the bears! Nanook is the god of retribution!*"

He charged over and smashed the plastic box, sending the cassette spiralling, shooting its spool in a brown streamer.

There was a new crackle.

New but old.

The Grundig his grandfather had given him was on the bed.

"Lee, you there boy?"

"Stop!" Lee ran to the washroom, slamming the door behind him. He slid to the floor and rammed his fingers into his ears. Rational safety lived on the tip of a nail and that nail's effectiveness teetered on resumed silence. For minutes, the man kept his fingers rammed deep into his ear canals. The pain was horrid and wonderful. The ringing was a symphony of logical ache.

Fingers fell, tips blooded beneath the long nails. Lee drank from the sink, terrified the sounds would return as soon as he opened the washroom door. He inched it open, creeping like a cat. Quiet, a mess, *I'm insane.* He swallowed four Tylenol tablets as he looked out a window at the great black Arctic.

If nothing else, without communication or readings from Lee, the Eureka Station operators were due to come. The thought warmed and chilled simultaneously.

Only time now, he thought above the ringing sensation in his ears. Out the window, the Northern

Lights danced without forming maleficent images or glowing monstrosities. It was the visual miracle it always was and nothing more.

The scent from his body claimed his attention and Lee stepped away from the sky play and to the shower. "Only time, soon enough." He stood under the cool stream and drank as he bathed. His infected toe oozed.

He swept up glass and steel, put the broken machines back where they belonged and sat down feeling fortunate that he didn't destroy the television. Unsmiling, he watched comedies. One after another, Murphy, Williams, Murray, Candy, Hanks, Chase, Hawn.

~

Dangerfield dove from the highest plank on the screen and suddenly bright lights filled the world beyond the yard around the station. Lee stopped the movie and stared at the door as he dressed, refusing to take his eyes off the porthole and the light breaking through.

The door whooshed open. The noise of helicopter propellers sliced the quiet to pieces. A figure emerged from a shadow, bringing with him a great Arctic gust. The man dropped to fours and his parka became fur.

Lee shook his head and closed his eyes.

"Hello, Lee Henry?"

Lee smiled. He opened his eyes. A man, not a bear.

"Time to go, buddy."

He nodded, relieved, and followed the figure outside quietly wishing he could convey the relief without exposing how far gone he'd fallen. No matter. The new face was fine, sturdy. It was all in his head, *what a mess.* The helicopter was a little further than Lee originally thought and the chill nipped at his throat. Still, it was nothing. It was over and he was safe. Soon he'd be away from it all, well at least to Eureka until his replacement came.

Soon... *geez, this is a long walk.*

He tugged on the man's jacket who led him in the dark toward the light. The man stopped and turned. The simple question *why land so far away?* went unasked, and yet, was answered.

The man leaned in. He smelled of fish and decay. "Nanook," he whispered.

"What?" Lee shouted over the whipping helicopter blades.

"Nanook!"

"I don't—"

The man disappeared. As did the lights. The whipping blades were nothing more than normal winds. Lee spun, terrified. So far into the distance was a pinhead of light.

The station compound.

Pain climbed on his bones like vine on brick. His naked body shined under the moonlight. He opened his mouth to speak, cold air rushed into his throat and lungs.

The wind sang above the damage he'd done to his ears. There were no more words or accusations.

Lee dropped to his knees. The Arctic floor was rough glass against his skin. Everywhere, all around him, the fishy scent reigned like fresh cut grass during suburban summer or spread cow manure in the spring countryside. Bears circled and sat in wait for their next meal to cease movement.

Lee wheezed and cried into his palms. The wind spoke, "Nanook. Nanook. Nanook."

Dead Lake

The price was right, and Carla Cohen understood what a price like that typically meant. She didn't need a fixer-upper, not at that point in the game. But the place met and exceeded her expectations, sidestepping the typical.

"Lake's no good for swimming, can't go in. Some fish manage I think, but I wouldn't eat them," the realtor said, an ex-athlete according to his size and strength. The belly bulge overhanging the belt buckle suggested the ex part of the equation. "That's why it's so darn cheap."

The honesty was nice to hear, Carla expected some *get it while it's hot* and a little *at this price, it won't last* kind of spiel, but it didn't come. It was plain old honesty and that the lake, what should've been cottage's main attraction, was what kept the place on the market and the price low.

"Oh, some pollutant then?" Carla asked.

"That's right, but it's a darn mystery. The owner, poor guy, the last realtor that sold him the place didn't mention the problem, a big no-no. That realtor should *lose his mother-loving license*. 'Scuse my language. I don't care for cheaters. I don't like sneaky cheaters at all."

Carla smiled at the man. Those weren't exactly harsh words. "Goddamn right, to hell with cheaters."

The realtor smirked uneasily. Carla wondered if he was the religious type, and found humor in a man of such a size so easily offended.

"As far the cottage goes, it's winterized, but it can get sticky here. So if you do like it enough to buy it, after October I'd be sure you had enough supplies to carry you through for a month."

"Is that right?" Carla began to walk back toward the cottage. The water in the lake looked fine. Carla didn't swim and didn't care to tease the fish with wading toes.

Carla had had a single swimming lesson. Her father launched her into a shallow lake when she was small. She climbed out with three leeches clung to her legs and wailed as if someone cut off an arm. She never took to swimming, never *accepted* another lesson.

At some point, you're either in the game or on the sidelines, and as far as enjoying water bound activities went, she was a connoisseur of the bench board.

"There's a woodstove and a bit of the forest comes with the cottage. You'll be the only cottage on the lake, so you don't have to worry about noise. What is it that you do, Miss Cohen?" the realtor asked as the pair walked around the side of the cottage to show an ancient pile of wood next to a fire pit.

"I produce music."

"Whoa, you related to Leonard Cohen?"

Carla shook her head, silly question. "I don't think so."

"Oh, I like Leonard Cohen. So what do you think? About the cottage, I would give you a whole story about other buyers, but I…" he trailed.

"You don't want to cheat me. Just tell me, is there a smell?"

"A smell?"

"Yeah, a smell from the lake, in the air I mean?"

"Oh, no. Only if you go in. It was quite a shock to the current owner's wife who went in. She was sick and died shortly after. Sad stuff. Oh, also, there's a caretaker through the bush. I could introduce you, he'll know more about the place, but it's nothing major as far as I figure. 'Spose I could call him and get back to ya. Now that I think about it—"

"Don't worry. Just give me his name and number. I'll call him. I trust you have the paperwork ready. I was going to low ball when I figured the place was ready to collapse, but since it's only shitty water, I'll pay the ask."

The realtor held out a hand. "Very good!"

The realtor left and Carla dialed the number for the former caretaker, former as soon as she'd purchased the place. She assumed she'd need only occasional help, there was likely something he could do, but nothing full-time.

The call failed and the crossed out signal bars explained why. It was landline/satellite phone kind of area. Carla opened every window. The place had that cleaned up smell, like pine and vinegar. She looked out, facing the lake. "This is it," she said, "this is retirement." It was a nice idea, spending time with nothing but a view. The closest town was more than forty-minutes away. She had an untainted piece of heaven all to herself, untainted so long as she stayed out of the lake.

Carla didn't spend the night, would've liked to, but couldn't. She took the southbound highway, the only one available for a huge swatch of Ontario, and rolled for a solid clip back to her condo. The trip took six hours.

Once home she rested, readied her weary body for the act of packing. It was just her, so it could've been worse. No kids, no significant other, only one woman's stuff. How things had gone, that was for the best.

~

After the two hired packers left, Carla fell down onto her bed one last time in the condo before the move to the lake. She was asleep by eight, the sky dim, but an hour or more from dark. She dreamed of her new home.

She dreamed of neighbors, smiling children, busy swimmers, and nosey raccoons, and rats. She dreamed of snakes.

Siss-siss-sick's how we like'm, a snake said with a child's face. It was silly, so obviously impossible that despite the sinister nature, it bothered her none. Dreams are dreams and nothing more.

Carla's eyes opened to find morning. It was time to move on.

A little after six, she was on the road, coffee in hand. The plan was to purchase groceries before she left, enough for a month, although winter was still weeks away, even by the early northern timeline.

Shopping for the cottage gave her giddy butterflies and she shuddered as the case of Campbell's Tomato went into her cart. Buying everything by case offered another first to go with all the lasts she'd left behind.

She put an eight-roll pack of Charmin into the car, a year's worth typically, and a six-pack of Bounty, that she'd use up getting that awful vinegar smell off everything. Cleaning would be a chore and she thought of the windows, the yard, the lake, and then remembered her dream snake.

Did cleaning matter much at all?

The little piece of paper was in her wallet and she fished it free. The windows were still open, airing the place out, and if her dream were any kind of omen or prophecy, a mess of water would get inside.

The paper said *Theo - Caretaker* and beneath that was his telephone number. Carla dialed and after four rings, heard an automated machine.

"Hello, Mr. uh, Theo. I am just checking in. I purchased the cottage at the lake and left the windows open and was wondering if it might rain, that you might go close them for me. Also, I would like to keep you on for—" She paused, thinking of a nice way to fire someone she'd never hired, never met, and knew nothing about. It wasn't a conversation for the telephone and she refocused. "I will be there in about seven hours and would like to meet you, if possible. Thank you." She was about to hang up. "Oh, my name is Carla Cohen." She hit end and continued shopping, the butterflies transformed into moths and chewed at her insides.

~

Half-awake, Carla hummed along with the radio as she drove. The GPS on the dash suggested that she was down to ninety-nine kilometers until departing the highway. The radio fuzzed and she tuned through stations. She listened a few seconds and hit seek, watching the numbers flip and then stop. She repeated the step several times through the limited northern options.

Carla let her eyes follow the numbers like a lazy fly gliding circles around a shit heap. The number flipped and changed, finding mostly empty airspace. A pop rock song blared, mixing horridly with the static.

She glanced up to the road in time to see trouble. Elk skittered across the asphalt in a pack. Automatically, she swung the truck into the oncoming lane and found the shoulder. The brakes thudded and tugged, but the gravel denied hold and the truck went over. Carla's head smacked the steering wheel. Glass shattered in a crystal shower and the airbag blasted her backwards.

The world was silent. The elk picked a side and munched grass a little ways from the road and the mess. Carla fell and floated to and fro from conscious to unconscious. Water dribbled in the window and she attempted to close the gap. The button refused to push the glass any further.

For the blurry moments awake, she arrived at the decision that she was only minutes from death. It felt just as well. Her time was limited, more limited than the average, more limited than most in a flipped truck.

"Let me sleep." She tasted blood.

A scream was beyond her status and the concussion borrowed her from the world for two hours until a truck rolled along, willing to dial nine-one-one, but unwilling to wait. Forty more minutes passed and finally a police cruiser and an ambulance found the overturned Honda Ridgeline. The pack of elk was long gone.

It wasn't so bad. The truck was a write-off. Carla had a few good noggin bumps and a dislocated shoulder. If it wasn't for her two shattered knees, she could've walked away as soon as she woke up, that and recovered her capacity to understand her body in space after the intense rattling of her brain.

"Don't worry lady, you're gonna make it," a foggy face said. There was a lot of hubbub, but they finally cut the belt and let her body fall into their cradling arms. Two men worked at the task of live body retrieval.

It was eighty kilometers back to the hospital, one hundred forty kilometers south, from the cottage.

~

After hearing the message, the caretaker looked into the bright and cloudless afternoon sky. He frowned thinking about what exactly a new owner might entail and continued to peer over the animal life scurrying about his shack in the woods. He didn't care to answer the telephone. It wasn't really why he was out there, year after year, decade after decade.

The day moved on, Theo listened for an approaching vehicle and when he didn't hear anything but the natural world, he lifted his watch to his ear. He waited three additional hours and decided to take the short trip through the woods to the lake and the cottage.

The water was lifeless, a space between times of breathing and death. He entered and closed all the windows in case it rained overnight.

~

"On top of everything else…" started the doctor. Carla waved off the statement, she didn't want to rehash any bad news. "Right, well, you've had a concussion, a few cuts and abrasions, but it's your legs that'll cause you the most grief, on top of everything else, that is." The doctor couldn't help it and shuffled his paperwork, avoiding eye-contact.

"How long until I'm back on my feet?"

The doctor looked up from his busy hands and into Carla's gaze. "Hard to say, I mean…"

"Got it," Carla said.

"Do you have someone?"

Carla almost laughed at the question, as she did have someone, sort of. A strange idea really, she didn't know the man, but assumed it was possible to pay for any hand that she might need. The doctor continued to gawk, and then, suddenly, as if given orders via earbud, made busy of a clipboard and stepped from the room.

Looking down at her legs, "Pretty typical move," Carla said and laughed.

~

It was sixteen days after the expected arrival date. The only extra on the Plain Jane wheelchair was a reclining back. It made a world of difference when it came to weight distribution.

Two men from the moving company salvaged what they could. The crash claimed the television and some dishes, but the sound equipment made it.

It was going to be boring stuck on her ass.

"Oh the joys of retirement," Carla mused to the scruffy man that approached, a pipe dangling from his lips. "You must be Theo?"

"Tay-yo." His touch ran over the hardened plastic in his mouth and then gave Carla a handshake.

"Right, well, I was wondering if you'd stay on and help, especially now that I'm indisposed."

"Ain't goin' nowhere."

"That's good, because I'm going to need a ramp." Carla hadn't thought it through and spoke while she looked around—too many non-wheelchair ready surfaces.

"I can do'at."

"Great. Where do you live, by the way?"

Theo pulled his pipe from his teeth and pointed into the woods.

Carla nodded. Her attention drew away from the man and to the movers. She'd never seen men paid an hourly wage work at such a pace. It was a Friday afternoon pace on a Wednesday morning.

"I'd best get inside and give some guidance, seems these fellas have fire in their veins. Would you mind helping me up the steps and through that door?"

Theo had already started pushing the wheelchair and rather than rolling backwards one step at a time, the scruffy man lifted the chair as if woman and machine were nothing more than Styrofoam forms.

"Oh, hey, thanks, you're stronger than you look." Carla clung to the chair. Theo gave a last little push and Carla rolled along. "Seriously, thanks a lot, do I need to…" she turned to find Theo was already moving towards a small out building halfway between the cottage and the lake.

"That's it," a young man said, sweat dripping from his brow.

Carla looked at the boxes and her furniture scattered willy-nilly. "Excuse you? Like hell it is. I paid for the deluxe service and since I can't move, you're not going to shirk this one."

"Sorry lady, you'll get a partial refund, I'll see to it, but we're not stickin' around this place."

As the one man spoke, the other man shook his head.

"Bull, how am I supposed to move this stuff?"

"Sorry," the man said, and he and his partner hurried out the door.

Carla ran fingers through her straight auburn hair. The fresh air mingled with the dulled shampoo scent that lingered behind a layer of sweat. A headache was around the corner, surely to accompany it, Carla's legs would start to wail and her stomach would revolt when she took another painkiller.

There were a good number of shelves and cupboards in the cottage and Carla could reach fewer than half of them. She unpacked what she could, taking breaks often, and an hour after starting, she wheeled over to the bay window overlooking the water. There, she tilted the chair back and attempted a nap. At first, it seemed as if there was no way in the world that the pain was willing to lessen enough for sleep, but sleep came. When she awoke, she awoke to straggling grey hairs over her shoulder.

"Whoa, oh hey."

The caretaker straightened his back. "I's jus' checkin'."

Checking what? "All right?"

"You gonna need some changes 'round, you want'm done?"

Changes? You're a strange old kook. "What changes?"

"I ain't gonna lift you on'ta the turlet, gonna need a bar. Gonna need a shower seat."

Carla hadn't thought of those problems and nodded at the bushman's thoughtfulness. Theo went outside and Carla followed as far as the door. There was a ramp waiting. It had some kind of granite roofing tape on it for traction, a smooth banister, and a gentle slope. It seemed impossible that this man had constructed it in the short time. Carla rolled down into the gravel. Her wheels made small divots, but nothing she couldn't manage, even with a sore shoulder.

"That's great, you do great…" she started to say, but found the caretaker had already moved beyond earshot. Carla gave a turn and rolled backward up the ramp. It was like work, and pain shot through her legs, a fuzzy Nurse Ratched's voice floated into her head, *medication time, medication time*. Early or not, she was due.

Theo moved in and out of the house without saying anything, working hard and working fast.

Musing under a blanket of dope, Carla thought perhaps that Hard-n-Fast Labor would make a fine title for the man's business. If he looked after more than one home.

~

It was dark and for a single second, Carla attempted to stand before recalling useless limbs. She wheeled to a light switch and felt around the wall. It was right where she'd left it.

Hunger invaded and she rolled to the fridge. The interior reminded her of the accident and the delay. The cool breezy scent matched the produce section of the Superstore where she'd typically shopped, before. That was all it resembled concerning edibles.

All of her perishables had met the inside of a garbage

can before their time and she had an empty fridge but for condiments and a jar of pickled chili peppers. She reached for the jar, it was cold and the lid and walls had stood their ground against the crash, protecting her pepper cache. There was a satisfying pop, the pickled smell filled the air in the quiet cottage. Carla jammed a fat pepper between her lips and put the jar back into the fridge.

At the hospital, they fed her tasteless imitation foods. The pepper brought flavor home to the sensitized area. Her lips burned while she wheeled to another cupboard and found soda crackers.

No television, she plugged the stereo together. There were a handful of discs left. She'd lost many in the crash. Which was but a temporary problem for the work she'd done, if she ever wanted to correct it with a series of phone calls, someone at the studios would burn her new copies. But why bother? It was not the stuff she worked on that she really liked to hear anyway, not alone. She filled the aged changer and listened the *Top Gun* soundtrack.

It made her want to dance. That made her frustrated. She punched at the armrests of her chair along to the beat. It helped.

In a box with the stereo equipment was the rest of her electronic toys and the anger subsided when she found the night vision goggles she'd purchased from a company online. When they arrived, there was a fat scratch over the right lens, but it didn't matter anyway since she'd bought them assuming them a half-assed, over-priced gag. Besides, she hadn't found the time to leave town and try the things out in the wilderness. "Until now." She flicked the living room light switch and then the kitchen switch before settling the chair at the bay window.

The world where she lived in a wheelchair drifted

away and she watched the green landscape, a whole lot of nothing. A moth bounced on the window and appeared massive, startling Carla at first, but since it was the only thing to see, she tapped the window and watched the flapping dusty wings. The moth settled, she tapped again and rather than fluttering against the glass, it fell. Beyond the tight gaze, Carla recognized the slim silhouette of a tall deer, or elk walking shakily into the lake.

"Oh wow."

The deer stepped until its motion was smooth. Swimming. It approached center. Carla blinked and in that second, the deer disappeared, leaving only ripples heading to the shores.

She waited for the animal, or if nothing else, for the corpse, to rise. Nothing came of it.

~

Carla awoke around ten and didn't see the caretaker until the afternoon. She wondered how much she owed the man for his trouble. Pointless thought. Theo was worth whatever he'd ask.

The air was nice and cool, she opened the windows and let the music ride the country. It was loud, but not so loud that she didn't hear a knock at the door. It was Theo—who else?—and he'd come to ask for a grocery list.

"Great, how much do I owe you so far?"

"Whutchever you see fit."

"You must've had a string of honest employers. How long have you been caretaker here? Was it just the last guy?"

"The last was a man and woman, woman died and the man tried to own the land, but'cha can't own Dead Lake."

"I guess that's right. Waterways belong to everyone or something. So how long have you been caretaker?"

she reiterated, as Theo's age was an unimportant mystery, the kind that pokes and annoys every time it crosses a mind. He was much older than Carla and Carla wasn't exactly a ripe young woman anymore.

"Long'nuff."

"Right, so do you need cash or card for the groceries? I guess it'll be a hike. The nearest store is what, fifty-K?"

Theo took a leather satchel from his pocket and loaded his pipe. The hard tip clanked on his teeth and Carla understood that an answer wasn't about to come.

"Right, well I can write a list and you just—"

Theo shook his head. "Jus' spill, I'm old, but I'll 'member."

Carla gave a list, leaving off much since she didn't want him to forget the necessities.

~

Impossibly, a knock came at the door only a little more than an hour after the last. Carla opened and allowed Theo to enter with four large burlap sacks in hands. The first three had everything she'd mentioned and the fourth had all the things she left off the list.

Carla watched in amazement. It was there on her tongue, the demand to ask how the man knew, ask where he got his money, ask how old he was, ask why he helped, but instead she said, "I saw a deer last night. It walked into the lake and drowned, I guess."

Theo didn't stop and continued arranging the groceries within Carla's shortened reach. The freezer posed an annoyance, as did the oven, but Theo moved the microwave onto a chair so Carla could heat burritos and pizza bagels, two things she hadn't mentioned, but wanted and now had anyway.

"It was strange, I've never heard of such a thing. Is that why you call it Dead Lake? The realtor had a different name, an Aboriginal thing I think."

"Lake Atinopin." Theo stacked the bottom of the fridge. "Same idear."

"Hmm, interesting. Did it get that name because the deer drown in the lake? Is that what makes it stink?"

"Don't stink."

"That realtor told me…"

"Don't stink, don't stink like ya think. Ya go in, you better be ready to go in. Ya almost ready?"

Carla wondered what the man played at, but figured he meant the casts. "I never had much of a sea leg before the casts. I won't go in. I have a phobia of fresh water."

"Dead Lake knows when you ready, try get ya before though."

Theo's first downfall was almost comical. Dead Lake sounded very much like an old timer's fishing tale, tall as the hills. "How did you know what I wanted for groceries, besides the ones I asked you to bring me?"

"The accident," Theo said.

"The accident?"

"Ya had your things when ya smuckered yer truck."

That was so much more reasonable than a mind-reading caretaker. Carla laughed heartily.

~

The drugs helped with the sleep. Carla went to bed early most nights and slept through until morning. Some days she saw Theo, others she didn't. On the days she wanted him, the man showed up, as if conjured by thought.

By the second week at the cottage, Carla had an idea and spent the morning thinking about Theo. A little after lunch the man appeared. There were more chores. He first screwed a wide stool together beside the stove before moving on. It was like watching an Amish master craftsman. The tools were archaic but looked mint. Within minutes, Carla saw her notion of a stove ramp come to life. Unfortunately, the fridge door wouldn't flip, but it was already infinitely more accessible than before.

Theo left, ignoring Carla's offers to fix him supper. Carla cooked a massive lasagna nonetheless. It was while she ate a second piece that a coughing fit began. The doctor said it would likely show at the beginning with a harsh, dry cough.

Here it was.

The cough subsided and the following night, she awoke, despite the painkillers, choking on a dry scratch that began deep in her throat. She climbed into the chair, slamming her legs against the frame. It hurt, but not as it had before. She hacked and tasted blood, rolled to the kitchen for a drink. She drank until she didn't feel the urge returning. Unfortunately, it killed any chance at rest.

The night vision goggles sat on a table near to the bay window. She dimmed the lights and watched the lake. Her gaze found life immediately. There were people floating, swimming in the lake. She dropped the goggles and felt around the floor with desperate fingers. She scooped up the goggles and held them slightly askew. The swimmers had turned to look at the cottage. Glistening skin glowed in the moonlight.

She nearly dropped the goggles again. "No fuck," she whispered. "No fuck."

One at a time, the heads dropped below the water. It was just like the deer, the lake rippled, but no bubbles of life rose to surface. Somewhere in the back of Carla's brain, the notion of hallucination began to trickle tendrils of demanded logic, until the swimmers' heads all approached her piece of shore.

"No fuck."

She stopped counting at twenty as they trudged up the lawn. Carla picked up the cordless telephone, enlivening the glowing green buttons. The last owner put Theo's number in the first autodial slot. She hit *AUTO* and then *ONE*. Carla listened to ringing. A knock hit her door. The loud thud filled the air and she dropped the goggles and the phone.

"Dammit all!"

Someone tested the door's lock. Carla didn't remember setting the lock but thanked herself for doing so. Another set of knocks rocked the peaceful silence.

"Get outta here. Leave'r be, she ain't for ya. Not yet. Go'way!" Theo's familiar voice yelled outside.

Carla was too scared to look out the window and waited for more knocks, but none came. Minutes passed, Carla decided to try the window. She tapped around the floor, first finding the phone and then finding the goggles. She lifted them to her face and saw a silent lake, nothing else.

Theo wasn't out where she could see and she decided to try the phone again. It rang until an automatic message connected. The cough began and forced Carla's focus away. She sipped at water, the morphine lollipops the doctor gave her on the way out of the hospital would make an agreeable side dish.

The world went fuzzy quickly and logic tendrils found more homes, stronger grips. It had to be the medicine, there was no way she saw people in the lake and she doubted a yelling caretaker would send them running.

~

She had coughed while she slept. The Rorschach splotch of blood on the pillow was proof. *Things would go fast once they started.* Carla wiggled her toes when she rolled onto her back, thinking about her legs and how ridiculous it all was. Thinking she'd planned a good retirement made her laughed humorlessly.

She slid onto to the chair and wheeled to the bathroom. She'd gotten used to pissing with her legs stuck out like planks, but the mornings could be tricky. She thought about the lake while she sat and what had to be a hallucination. If it wasn't, *where did they all come from? What did they want? What did Theo say to get them to leave?*

"She ain't for you," Carla said to the cramped bathroom. "That's what he said."

She strong-armed her way from the toilet seat to the chair and rolled out through the kitchen to the door. The lock wasn't set. *One point for the hallucination*, she thought. She searched the area around the lake for footprints and found nothing; *a second point for the hallucination*. She wheeled up the slope from the lake, at that moment wishing she had neighbors that shared the pond. She returned to the ramp.

"Hmm," she said, seeing a dirty smudgy handprint on the door. Bits of mud and dried brown streams of murky water ran from the spot. Even from where she sat, there was an obvious scent. It was earthy and natural. She leaned in for a stronger, closer whiff.

Not quite earthy.

It was decay, rotting and sweet, like an apple turning to brown mush. She sniffed again and the scent transformed, *maybe it isn't rot after all*. She took a third snout-full.

"Flowers and ozone." She sat back and then leaned in again. "Ugh, Christ." The print had mixed up her olfactory senses because she once again smelled rot and decay, even a hint of ethanol fume.

The logical explanation behind the handprint was Theo. It didn't matter what the smell was. Smells come from everywhere.

Smells.

She whiffed her shirt.

She hadn't showered in three days because it was a pain in the ass and the legs. It was a procedure to strip, bag her casts, and climb onto the shower stool, one that took close to an hour.

The Glad garbage bags over her legs looked ridiculous, but she didn't have a choice. The doctor said she'd have to come back after ten weeks, but they may need to stay on for up to eighteen weeks.

While bending to remove the bags, Carla's lungs compressed and she began the worst coughing fit she'd experienced yet. Her entire body ached, and after gasping for two straight minutes, she opted for another lollipop. The drug put her into a comfortable state for the shower.

~

Still damp, the world came back to Carla, a rotting sense rose in her gut. It was the morphine. Folding away the day, twilight verged on Carla, leaving her confused and disheartened. With every spin of the globe, the looming hopelessness weighed more and more.

She heated a soggy pizza from the fridge. "We can't always get what we want." She watched the pizza through the oven's golden baked window.

The coughing fits came on now and then, but she managed to understand how many licks it took and when water alone would do. She sat looking out the window with the stereo blasting at full volume until night consumed the shapes. Moving rarely, she continued listening to music, she let the changer spin through the rock, the pop, and the rap. Even with the lights on, the inside of the cottage seemed as dark, if not darker, than the black night outside.

The pity bubbling within finally reached the brim and spilled over. Carla put her hands to her face and cried. A bout with the cough commenced, halting her woeful tears, exchanging them for physically pained ones. Then she heard it, just barely, not over but through the music, a knock at the door. She rolled to the stereo and lowered the volume.

"Hello?" She thought about the creepy swimmers. "Who's there?"

Another knock.

Carla raced to the window. She lifted the goggles. The world outside the window looked normal.

"Who's there?" She side-eyed the door.

Three quick and loud raps landed.

"Who is there?"

She gave the outside another peek and decided to fight this irrational fear. She rolled to the door.

Another knock seemed to pound into every corner of the cottage, threatening to burst eardrums and shatter glass.

Carla covered her ears, waited, and then affronted her fear and threw open the door.

"Who—oh?"

"Heya, ma'am," a small girl said, soaking wet black hair, a scummy plaid shirt, and jeans and a flower barrette above her right ear. Three petals had broken away, but the four remaining suggested a sunflower.

"Who are you?" The child seemed so familiar.

"I'm Jesse, a course, and you're Carla Cohen."

"What are you doing out here?"

"I came to say hi. We all wonder 'bout you. How come you never come swimmin'?"

"I don't swim, do you want something to eat or drink? Should we call your parents?" Something wasn't quite right, it didn't *feel* as if her parents would see her absence unusual.

"Can't eat and swim. I'll get all crampy. How come you don't swim? Nobody never teach you?" The girl pulled a soggy pack of Bubble Yum bubble gum from her pocket. It was dirty and the gum inside the wrapper was greenish pink rather than rosy pink. She put the pack in her pocket and popped the green gum into her mouth. She blew a bubble. It was hideous and continued to grow like a sunbaked frog's throat.

"Should I call your mom?" Carla was unable to think of something more befitting the oddity. Rationale demanded reason.

The bubble popped and thick slime of green and black lake bottom splattered onto Carla's chest. "Oops, sorry 'bout that, ma'am. You should come with me. We know you sick, we don't care. We was all sick one way or 'nother."

"Go away, away!" Theo yelled from the forest, the sound of his footfalls approaching let Carla breathe easier.

"See ya later." Jesse jumped from the high side of the ramp.

"Take this back wit'cha." The ejaculation from Theo's shotgun gave reason for the birds to fly and the nightlife to go silent but for the echoing sound of the buckshot spray.

"Eat it," she said, as if that rifle shot nothing more than glitter, and ran towards the water. Theo aimed, but didn't bother with another shot.

Carla watched in disbelief, the holes the buckshot made oozed with reflective black mud, but didn't slow the girl. She jumped into the water, swam toward the center and then sank. No bubbles rose. A gentle ripple rode the surface.

"What's going on?" Carla tried to demand but her tenacity faltered and true emotion appeared. "Please."

"Why'd ya move here?" Theo asked, his voice its typical drone.

"I retired. I wanted to get away."

"How'd ya hear 'bout the place. You's sick, int'ya? Int'ya? That's why ya come, last guy was a good'un. His wife was sick, but he didn't sell fer a long time."

"The realtor said it was on the list for years."

"Might'a bin, but he wasn't tryin' to sell. He was hopin'. Fer a while he talked to his wife, but she couldn't get'm to go in. He knew better than to swim in Dead Lake. Some put they heart after they brain, but not'm. He wuddn't sick, wuddn't ready fer a dip. Yer pretty sick, int'ya?"

Carla wanted to roll back inside and bury her head in morphine pillows. She couldn't say the words. The doctors had said the words, but she never could. She retired and that was the easy part, everyone knew she was single without expenses, one that made good money and lived like a frugal old spinster. People expected her to retire and she never had to say it. She hadn't spoken to her parents in decades. Carla Cohen had nobody to reason realities with but herself, and she refused.

Saying it meant it was certain. The lollipops, the pills, the painkiller drip in the hospital, the scans, the x-rays, none of it, none of it was real until she said it. Carla didn't answer and rolled back through the door.

~

Carla awoke on the couch. There was a demand in her bladder. Her head was still foggy, that girl's face looming. She reached for the chair, shifted her weight and grew weak. The floor came at her like a rising elevator. Her body thumped and pain tore through her legs. Her chest heaved and a hacking cough began. The fight was on, she clenched to hold in piss, to climb into the chair, ignore the cough, and deal with the external pain.

The strength in her arms faltered twice more before she got into the seat. A rotten, empty feeling joined the screaming bladder and she raced to the bathroom. Her arms didn't fail this time and found the cold off white of the toilet seat. She pulled her pants away further and let the stream go.

It ached and burned. Tears fell from her eyes as her

urethra blazed. She squeezed off for a brief reprieve, but it only made things worse. She coughed and the piss flew, splashing her vagina lips and her thighs. She coughed hard until vomit belted from her rotten gut.

"Thank God," she said as the stream ceased and the burn subsided. The puke mostly hit the garbage pail next to the toilet. Her pants had a big wet stain. Instead of pissing onto her casts, she'd pissed on her tear-away pants.

The tears streamed and she put hands to cheeks. It was a short-lived bout with pity and she tossed the pants at the hamper and rolled to the kitchen. The morphine lollipops sat in a low cupboard and Carla swung it open to find a score of dead rats and chewed plastic around the medicinal treats. She'd noticed animal nuggets, just little ones, here and there since moving in, but thought little of it. Seeing her drug stash ruined by furry beasts made her tears rise with new force. She punched the cupboard doors until her knuckles bled.

"Guy's wife, last owner, she was sick too," Theo said. He stood in the doorway. "She stepped out and come home sick. AIDS. Fella 'fore that had big ol' feet, puffy and sick. 'Fore him was a family, the kids was all short and limped, they had spots too. Sick, sick, sick, all'm sick. Dead Lake calls'm out. The lake wants'm to give up, but ya never know, things change. The lake eats hope and holds all the rest. Ya wanna go, ya should go someplace else, not into the lake."

Carla thought about it, thought about her reflection and thought about how wrought she looked, how deflated she felt. She turned to tell Theo to *fuck off*, but Theo was gone, leaving behind only a boot print and some hokey wives' tales about the lake.

"Eats hope? To hell with hope!"

Naked from the waist down, Carla opened every window, maxed out the stereo volume, and rolled down to the lake. She sat looking at her reflection. Harmless flies landed on her bare thighs to lap up errant piss before buzzing away. By twilight, black flies took the place of their harmless brethren, but they didn't bite, as if they recognized that her blood was not good blood.

"They don't want anything to do with me," Carla mused, swatting at the circling annoyance. "Me neither."

"There's always a chance," Theo's voice came like a dull drumbeat. He'd managed to sneak up again. He carried the shotgun. "There's always room fer hope."

"What are you doing here, Theo?"

"I come see if ya need somethin'. That's all."

"No, what are you doing here, why are you at Dead Lake?"

"I come a long time ago, I's sick too, but I fought it, didn't want to go with'm in the lake. I come for the lake, but changed my mind. Two owners ago, he called it limbo. I's in limbo and can't go nowhere no more. The lake takes'm sick and keeps'm that way. The woods keep me, provide all I needs, but I ain't so sick no more, less I leave. No need, there's magic in'm woods just like there's magic in'at water."

It was stupid and unreasonable. "Couldn't have been too sick." Carla was willing to wage any pissing contest about being sick Theo might want wage.

Theo shrugged. "Sick as I gets, family got it too. They's gone. The lake likes'm sick."

Carla didn't respond and Theo sat down on the shore next to the wheelchair. The shotgun clanked on a pebble and Carla, who suspected as much, felt uneasy knowing the rifle was there. Theo looked at her as if about to hand over the weapon and suggest an alternative action.

The rotten sensation ensued with rebounded force. A coughing fit sent racked echoes over the lake.

Dusk became night and overhead the stars twinkled and blazed with amazing lividness. It was unlike anything she could remember seeing. Even in areas of low population, the pollution seemed to waft and dwell overhead: light pollution and air pollution, both dampen the stars. Carla marvelled as if seeing them for the first time.

"I can understand why you stay, I guess."

"There always a chance. And if ya goin', ya don't wanna go in the lake."

Soundlessly, heads surfaced on the black surface, approaching the shore. Carla heard the readying of the shotgun. Angry, she reached down and squeezed his shoulder. They weren't there for him.

"No. I have a cancer, it's inoperable and I'm as good as dead. It was too late when I found out." The admittance let all the rot flow from her nostrils and she was suddenly ready for something new, an unknown variable, an idea she'd never recognized but always took for granted before the doctor put a best before date on her ass.

"But ya ain't gotta go to the lake, go anywhere else. Get hope back or die clean, wit' no damned chains."

"It's not like that," Jess said, dripping and smiling under the starry night sky. "Come in, I'll teach you to swim."

Carla finally recognized her.

Siss-siss-sick.

Theo lifted the shotgun to the reaching shadow of a girl.

"Stop."

"But ya don't know, ya don't know nothin'," Theo pleaded. "It ain't good."

"Some things are worse than hanging on, Theo, some lives aren't worth it. But mine is and look, you say they're sick, but they're..." she said, trailing.

She attempted to stand on broken legs. The casts held, but her knees quaked and she went down.

"You ain't gotta walk to swim anyways," Jesse said stepping to the shore, reaching for Carla. "Why don't you come in too, Daddy?"

Theo ignored this, Jess wasn't his daughter, not anymore. "See, if it was good they'd help ya in, but they can't, the devil always gives the choice. We choose damnation, we choose to lose hope, we choose to fight the natural way."

Carla ignored him and crawled into the water. Jesse smiled and stuck out her tongue at Theo.

Immediately, understanding began to soak.

There was something wrong.

It was as if something invaded and pervaded her soul. Flailing, Carla gasped, changing her mind once in the cold water of sweet decay.

"No, I can't swim."

Theo shook his head and walked from the bank.

Carla attempted to claw and kick, moved inch by inch in the wrong direction until the water rose above her head, gulped the nasty sludge and it filled her veins from the lungs out, pushed up and turned, realizing her error and fought with inept strokes in the opposite direction.

The lake keeps ya, Theo had warned her.

Jesse swam through the murk and kissed Carla on the nose as Carla sank.

"See, isn't swimming fun?"

~

There was near-silence for months.

"Hello mister," a low voice said and Theo looked down at the bald child. The child's parents busied themselves with boxes, a big move, the whole family needing a change of scenery at a rock bottom price.

"Reckon I could fix ya a rope'n tire swing, what ya think?" Theo offered a strained grin.

The child, not certainly male or female nodded and

smiled. "Can you make it swing over the lake like kids' on movies do? I love swimming."

Over the Fields and Through the Woods

There is no word that mutually describes sore, exhausted, and worried. Likewise with too young to know relentless stressors while simultaneously knowing them too damned well.

In the fields, the sun overhead worked at bubbling and peeling the skin from our necks. Clanking heavy rocks into the loader bucket fitted on the front of the ancient Minneapolis-Moline tractor, we worked like boys on an invisible chain gang.

That old machine was once yellow but sat in a state of flaking oranges and browns, rotten peach tones of oxidization and rust. Colors fading like our childhoods and displayed right before our eyes.

The un-yellowed paint wasn't alone, we'd been the color of Cheerios and became the color of tomatoes.

It was dirty work, field labor. A black rim of grime circled my mouth. I wiped and scratched at the gritty residue. Whenever I managed to get the caked dust-ring wiped away, more dust landed and ate up all the moisture, solidifying like paint. A black ring on a boiled red canvas.

I licked at my cruddy teeth and cracked lips, tasting all that our lives had become.

My brother Jake and me, tossing rocks from the field into the loader bucket. We weren't born into this life. It was bad luck that put us on the farm. Ah hell, it was downright shitty luck. The kind you see on the news and part of you wants to disbelieve stuff like this ever happens to kids.

Our mother had died two years earlier from lung cancer. I found that out later in life, back then I only knew something got her and ate her up from the inside out. There was no family left when she died and we went into the foster system. Home to home, trouble to trouble. Misfortune always finds some kids. It's magnetic, or something.

The first home that took us was all right. There was lots of food and the *mother* was nice, so long as we didn't break anything. There were four other kids there, at Ms. Kincaid's house. All girls, three younger than me, one older than me. Shelley was oldest, in high school, and she kept to herself. I spent a good amount of time imagining the freedoms of high school. It was only three years away.

The younger girls were the first case of bad business that found us. A gang of conniving mini-criminals ages seven, nine, and ten.

We were all foster kids at Ms. Kincaid's house and yet, the girls didn't like boys on *their* turf. It made it easy for the girls that Jake was always so forward and nosey. He liked to go into their rooms to ask questions and touch stuff. Jake always needed to learn things firsthand.

"Little pervert, I think. Girls say they caught him in their closet when they was changing, peeking on them with his hands in his pants. I'm sorry, but I can't do anything with them. You'd be smart only to send me girls here on out," Ms. Kincaid said into the phone.

I asked Jake and he asked me right back why he'd ever have his hands in his pants if he was hiding in a closet and looking at the girls change.

Nah, it was the perfect lie to send the opposite sex on the road.

A day later, we were boys with boxes looking at a new home. *Short-term*, that's what they said. Mrs. and Mr. Schwartz had too many kids as it was, mostly boys. Rough kids. They policed themselves while the Schwartz's collected the checks and then went to work at the printing press in town.

The first day was fine. We met everybody. A guarded niceness even peeked around the corners of their armor. It was different on the second day. Our new, temporary parents left for work and we learned about the pecking orders. We discovered how the bottom felt. We were the worms and there were birds circling overhead.

This was brief. The too tight living arrangements sent us on our way. Fine by me. Fine by Jake too. Or so we thought.

We went to a stinky old house, Mr. Benn's house. He had three dogs and only boys. Everyone was quiet and soft and Mr. Benn liked to give shoulder rubs and bath times. It was weird from the beginning.

Even old as I was, same as another boy, Mr. Benn used to demand that we bathe with the door open and all had to sleep in Boy Scout pajamas. My uniform was too small.

After a few months, Jake told me that Mr. Benn called him a dirty little boy. I asked what he was doing and he said, "Nothin', but he keeps on it. I don't like him."

This could've gone so much worse than it had. We

caught a lucky break, sort of.

Simon, one of the other boys, got sick and went to the hospital the night after one of Mr. Benn's milkshake parties. He'd give all but two of us boys milkshakes. The milkshakes were great and conked us right out. Two boys always had to stay up and *help* with the Mr. Benn's guests. Jake and me never got singled out to miss the milkshakes.

That last time Simon did and so did Robbie. The other boys told us that Simon almost always missed out on the milkshakes. The others explained this sadly and told us they couldn't tell us what the parties were like, just that *we'd see.*

Turns out, gonorrhea isn't any easy illness to explain away in a little boy.

The police came and took us out of there. Jake and me had no real emotional scars, while the other boys... shit. The bad turn put our names to the top of an adoption list. Like we were minor celebrity survivors of a horrible train derailment that sent most of the ticket holders under the dirt.

Jake prayed every night. He prayed to Mom instead of God, prayed she'd come back and save us. Back then, I wanted to slap him, explain the ways of reality. It's a hard world and I was learning, and so should he. I wanted to tell him, *Dead is dead, there's nothing after that. Dead is dead.*

Nathan and Emma Abbott adopted us and moved us to the farm.

They were monsters. Emma was a sharp-tongued drunk and Nathan was straight cruel, had a set of heavy fists. I remember the coin taste and black spots in my eyes like floating reverse halos when punches connected, seemingly out of nowhere.

The punches were short bursts, the opposite of the field in every way aside from the torment.

Jake clanked a stone near my head.

"Watch it, all right?" I said to him.

His skin seemed ready to curl off his back in great bubbles. If we burned anymore, I think we would've turned into raisins.

"Ya know, school should've started already. Must run different here, huh?" Jake said.

"I bet it already did start. I bet we don't get to go to school."

"No way. Not fair." Jake had a good-sized rock in his hand.

"I know, but we're slaves. You learn about slavery in school. Nathan and Emma own us, they adopted us, so they own us, and the police can't do nothing 'bout it. It's all legal, that's what adopted means, means nobody wants us unless we'll work all day." I thought, without doubt, that that was what adoption meant.

Often enough, I guess, that's exactly what it means.

"Bullshit." Jake fired his rock at the bucket.

The extra effort skewed his aim. He missed and hit a gummy steel coupler just above the word *Quicke* on the loader arm. Black liquid sprayed into the air.

"You dummy. You're gonna get it now," I said.

"No, no, it can't... I can fix it," Jake said, tears already spurting like desert springs.

It was a mess. It was all kinds of trouble.

"It's busted."

Bent metal wrapped around the cracked rubber hose.

Jake jumped up on one of the front wheels of the tractor and attempted to push the hose back together. The fluid continued its oily trickle. It had already pretty well painted Jake. Blackish stains like rainy clown mascara streaked his face.

We were so involved with the hydraulic hose that we didn't hear the steps coming from behind us. Nathan tossed me away from the tractor before I so much as sensed him.

"No, no, it was an accident, I swear. It wasn't my—" Jake started.

A fist into his mouth stopped his plea. Jake toppled from the tractor's wheel. Nathan looked at the hose, saw the bent steel, and recognized what happened. Carelessness.

"You no good, thankless little shit," he seethed through clenched jaw and grabbed at Jake's collar.

Jake rose from the ground and slid from his shirt. His back was so white it seemed to reflect light as if he was part mirror. Healing belt scars lined and crossed this fleshy plain. I didn't feel too bad for him. My back looked the same.

Nathan tossed the shirt away and went after Jake, who'd taken to scurrying on all fours. Dust floated on the air as Jake kicked for footing.

"Ungrateful little shit!" Nathan was a broken record, most hard drunks are.

His foot swung back and then flew forward into Jake's ass. Jake face planted into the dirt, taking a mouthful of soil on his first inhale.

"You can't do nothing right, ungrateful little shit!"

Nathan dropped to his knees and punched Jake in the back of the head with two swift pops.

By this point, I wanted to move, I swear I did, but if you've never witnessed a beating and felt absolutely helpless at the same time, you can't relate. As humans, we all pretend that if the time comes, if our number's called, we find our inner heroes. It doesn't work like that in me and I watched Nathan flip and pound my brother like he was pizza dough.

"This is how you repay me? I take you in and this is how you repay me? Ungrateful, thankless, little shit!"

Nathan landed two more shots into Jake's face and Jake stopped fighting. Limp in the dirt. Typically,

Nathan stormed away after a whooping and then I'd help my brother, but this was different. Nathan meant to hurt him in a way that would teach a lesson over and over again, forever. Nathan stormed toward me and a lightning fist connected with my forehead. I smelled metal, like batteries, and saw black. My body fell in slow motion.

Nathan kicked. "Ungrateful, both of ya!" His foot connected with my thigh and then my hip and then my arm.

The pain shot all over my body and I tried to cry out.

The kicks stopped and I opened my eyes, Nathan stood over me, his massive frame casting a horrid shadow. "Little shits, little shits! This is the thanks you give me? I didn't even get to plow your mama, but I get the thankless shits anyway!"

He dropped his knees into my chest and my body shrank. I gasped and dirty fists smacked, each hit offering a second of numb shock before the pain came.

"No, please," I begged, no sense pretending otherwise. Nathan kept at me and I squirmed to avoid direct strikes.

Then he fell forward, draped over me like a heavy damp blanket. A new shadow covered me. I looked up at my brother who held the same dirty stone that had busted the hose.

"You're gonna get it," I said, busted lip stinging, thinking Nathan was apt to get up and beat Jake senseless.

Jake leaned down to look, and Nathan turned sideways to look up.

"Thankless little—," he began anew.

Jake slammed that rock into the soft surface of Nathan's face nine more times.

He splashed as if playing in a red mud puddle.

"You killed'm!" I was so scared I thought I might

die of worry.

Jake tossed the rock aside and grinned. Glad at what he'd done. He'd saved his big brother and kicked some ass in the process.

"Come on, Austen, we gotta get out of here." Jake grabbed up his shirt and then he spat muddy blood.

"You can't just kill people, you can't. We'll get in trouble. He owned us. He adopted us, that's how it works. Oh you're in trouble."

"Not only me, come on. I don't want Emma comin'. I don't have no skid marks either, she's a liar. Come on."

I saw right then that my little brother had the hero stuff that I did not. I'll admit it irked me in a way that made me want to punch him silly. But I didn't.

We ran from the open fields of the farm to the neighbor's property, three hundred acres of flat, another two hundred of forest. We ran long and far, when we lost the energy to run, we walked. By evening, we came to the forest. It was probably no more than hour, but time's different when you're a terrified and on the run.

Jake had an uncanny way about the woods. I was a wreck. He led us right to the creek. Off and on all day I cried about what was surely coming for us. The punishment structure for bad kids that don't mind their adoptive parents was the kind of thing that had to scare even the hardest boys.

"What are we gonna do?" I whined.

I remember the scolding expression on Jake's face.

"Well, what?" I added.

"Umm, let's have a drink and think."

"Of what?" I shouted, not yet putting the gentle creek sound with the realization of water.

Jake pointed. Beyond a shrub was the two-foot-deep creek. It was cold and glorious. I drank until my belly hurt. Then I splashed away all the dirt and blood.

"Now what?"

Jake was still filthy. I wasn't in charge of keeping him clean so I didn't say anything.

"Umm, can we make a fire like on TV?"

It was and still is true that everyone that sleeps in the woods on TV builds a fire, but they also come prepared and I didn't have a clue.

"We don't got any matches. How can we start a fire?"

"Umm," he said and started walking.

We crossed the creek to a grassy shore on the other side. The reedy grass was long and Jake continued right through it, punching cattails. I was tired and hungry, my face stung, and I re-experienced each kick with every step I took.

Jake found a small clearing not far from the creek. It was sandy and the high grass offered us some shelter from the police that I was certain were out looking for us. I banged rocks and Jake rubbed sticks. We gave up after two minutes. The new plan was to spend the night cool and damp under the stars. Washing all the crud from our bodies opened the buffet doors for the mosquitoes. I slapped until I didn't care anymore.

I cried from hunger and fear. I cried from being cold and being who I was.

A howl stopped my tears. Jake crawled next to me, scared. We had no way of knowing how close the owners of those sounds were. Howling carries like little else when the moon is high and the night is quiet.

"I think they're close."

"You think?" I asked.

"The grass moved and I saw eyes, like a dog. What if it's wolves?"

I thought not. Coyotes were common. Wolves lived more north, like way up where there are lots of moose and bears.

"Scat!" I shouted. "Probably just coyotes," I

whispered into Jake's ear, hopeful.

The grass moved and a growl met us. My heart pounded.

Jake leapt to his feet and grabbed for my arm. "Run!"

Hand in hand, we sprinted. The sound of animals behind us fuelled our tired and haggard bodies beyond the bruising and sunburns and skitter bites. I could be wrong, I may have imagined it, but I was sure something nipped at my heels, toying with me. With us.

There was a tree ahead with a low branch and Jake steered us in that direction. The moon silhouetted the shape and made it seem to shine in the shadows. Onto that low-hanging branch, we climbed.

The limbs cradled us and we looked down, huffing and puffing at the sticky air. There they were, out of the shadows, eyes aglow yellow, teeth blinding white. Three of them, grey and tall, I didn't know much about coyotes, but I didn't think they got so big.

Jake was right.

Wolves, three wolves. They strode around the tree, taunting us. In the summer, there's food everywhere a wolf looks. These weren't normal animals. Normal, fed, summer wolves don't spy boys as if they're supper.

Right then I knew that because Jake had killed a man, these wolves had the task of doling punishment. I wanted to yell out pleas that it was Jake who got Nathan, not me. That I was just taking my licks when Jake came up with that rock, *it wasn't me at all!*

I dug my fingers into the dark wood and waited. Jake looked to the moon, ignoring the wolves.

"Mom, please help us. We won't be bad anymore. I swear we won't. Please, Mom, make'm go away."

"The dogs came to punish us and Mom is dead. It's 'cause you hit Nathan. Mom can't do nothing for us."

As I spoke, the wolves lost interest, or at least understood the game better than we did. Jake swore up and down that our mother saved us.

"See, see," he said making ready to jump from the tree.

"What are you doing?" I grabbed him.

"It's okay. Mom's protecting us."

"Like hell she is. She's dead and we aren't getting out of the tree until morning. It's dark and scary, we have to wait until morning, that way we'll see everything."

"Oh."

Jake wore a thinking face. He'd prayed to our mother often, but this was the first time I'd told him it was pointless.

"You don't think Mom can hear me?"

I shook my head. I don't know why. Right then it seemed of utmost importance to crush his sense of the afterlife.

"But, I… No, she hears me."

"No, Jake, Mom is dead. She can't help us."

"Nuh-uh, she's out there helping."

I can only say in my defense that I was overwrought and exhausted. I shook Jake and screamed, "Mom's dead! Mom's dead! She ain't helping shit!"

"Don't touch me." He jabbed two fingers into my chest.

I snatched at his fingers and Jake pulled back his arm. I twisted and he squealed. He was my brother and I wanted to hurt him for everything that had happened to us.

"Austen, please."

I let go and Jake fell backwards out of the tree.

I stared down into the gloom of the forest floor, there was a momentary silence and then Jake bellowed. "You're a jerk, I ain't getting' back in that tree!"

"Get back up here!"

He stared at me with glistening eyes and a filthy face.

Pained all over. He started walking. I had to jump down and try to convince him. I caught up to him and then I heard the steps in the grass, slow and close behind us.

"We gotta run, Jake," I whispered.

Jake took my hand and then took off. It was uncanny, his sense of direction. He led us through thick brush right onto a deer-run trail. The trail led straight to an old hunting cabin. It seemed like a desert mirage.

The wolves sensed the safety ahead of us. They snapped and snarled at our heels. I stumbled and Jake dragged me to my feet. I could almost feel the breath of those wolves, feel their teeth and their tongues, chewing me, savoring me.

"Come on, Austen!"

He pulled as I labored. We reached the cabin and I winced, knowing one was on me. Jake tossed open the door and threw me inside with a strength beyond his size and years. Adrenaline is something I did not learn about until much later in life.

It was pitch dark in there and smelled of smoke. None of that mattered. We were safe from the wolves. We leaned against the door and slid down to sit.

"Think they'll go away?" Jake asked.

"No," I said, my heart thumped a parade on my ribs, "they want us. They'll keep after us. Why did you do it? It's all your fault. You shouldn't have hit him. You killed him, Jake."

Jake whimpered. "He was gonna hurt you and he already hurt me. Mommy, please! Mommy, help us!"

"She's dead and dead is dead, there's nothing after that!"

The wolves began butting against the door. There was a thump and a whine with each contact. Then they'd run away only to charge back again seconds later.

"Mom can hear me. Why don't they just leave us alone?" Jake's words vibrated in his chest.

The door thumped.

A wolf snarled.

The door thumped again.

Another wolf snarled.

"Mommy, please!" Jake cried into his hands.

I was ready to slap him, on principle, how dare he not know the same things *I knew*, and believe the same things I believed. Instead of slapping him, my body went limp and anything I wanted to say sat dry in my throat.

Under the boarded window, a match struck out a blazing glow.

"Sounds like you boys are in some trouble," a gruff mannish voice said. It was something like a muffled chainsaw on concrete, set to language.

"Who are you?" Jake asked, his fear abated at the sight of the face floating in the black above the match.

The man lit a lamp and then a cigarette. He was old and dark. His skin looked almost blue or purple. Tattoos of bright oranges and reds danced, moving with the glow from the light, like florescent veins, luminescent blood.

"So yer killers, huh?" He smiled a mouth of shining yellowy teeth.

"Who are you?" Jake demanded.

"I killed plenty, ma'self," the man said.

"Who are you?"

I didn't utter a peep and moving was a foreign language. The man looked like a devil and I was some damn kid run out of luck. And yet, there was my little brother Jake, taking all the necessary stands. Fighting for two because his big brother didn't have the same heart to fight for himself.

"I died a few times too. Dead isn't dead, not always. Ya got that bit wrong, boy." The man laughed. "Sure, dead's only a matter of will."

His grin crawled over my back like army ants.

"Who are you?" Jake repeated.

"Who me? I ain't nobody important. Not like Austen."

"Me?" I croaked.

"Oh yeah, see, you got to face the punishment owed. You's killers, no matter who did the killin'."

He leaned forward into the light. The tattoos and veins wriggled frantically. He was a man of glowing snakes and worms and horrors.

"But it was Jake."

"Like I said, boy." The man blew out the lamp and only his cigarette and the colors on his skin remained aglow. "And you. Ya wanna know 'bout me? I come to make sure the toll's paid before anyone crosses the bridge."

Jake leaned into me. "Be ready to run," he whispered.

The devil before us made the wolves seem like stuffed animals. They hadn't banged in a while and I was willing to let Jake dictate my survival or my death. Thinking too much is a scary place.

Jake turned his focus back to the dark man standing above him. Little arms jerked out like a double-fisted gunslinger. He snatched the oil lamp and smashed its hot contents over the man's face.

The man cackled maniacally as the flames danced out from the cigarette spark, rolling about his skull, his wide eyes reflective pools that likely trailed back to the River Styx.

"Run!" Jake yelled.

I swung open the door, took two steps, and saw the world brightening all around me.

"Dead ain't dead, not always!"

Terror stole my strength. My legs refused movement, not one step more. There were the wolves and there was another man, just his silhouette in the shadow of a tree ahead, but I recognized him nonetheless. Nathan Abbott. Jake pushed at my back.

"Go, go."

The wolves growled, but refused to approach. It was all a part to the game. The toll we owed. They wanted us to run so they could chase. So fear filled our veins and made our meat reek of it while they lapped at the buffet.

"Dead is dead! Nathan is dead! Dead is dead!" I screeched as we ran.

"Keep moving. Please, Mom, help us! Help us!"

The gap between the trees shrank until we had to step sideways to get through. On the other side of the tree wall, a pond waited, a fog drifted from the cool air against the warm water. We'd never been any place like this before, but Jake... he understood.

"Come on," Jake pulled me toward the shore.

I thought that was it, game over. I couldn't swim and Jake couldn't swim. And yet, he dragged me over the muddy bank, looking toward the water. In the fog, a canoe floated, tied to a rotten wooden peg driven into the shore. It was too convenient. It was more evil, but we didn't have a choice.

We hopped into the boat as it shook, but never dipped far enough to take on water. I unravelled the rope and used one of the stark white paddles to push us adrift.

"Bones," Jake said.

"Huh?"

Then I got it. Bone paddles. I fought off another scream. How big was the monster who bore a paddle as a bone?

Jake stopped the effort and lifted his paddle from the water. I did the same, monkey see, monkey do, and from behind us, we heard it. Little splashes, the wolves swam. We didn't spot them yet, but felt fear enough as if we had.

Jake dropped his paddle back into the pond and

swung furiously. I mimicked him. We picked up speed. Wind whipped frozen air against us and my teeth chattered.

"What now?" A big puff of steam left my mouth.

It was snowing, in the middle of summer. *Snowing!*

"Do you hear that?" Jake asked.

I did but I had no answer as to the how or the what.

Jake turned toward me and for a heartbeat, I didn't see my brother, not as I knew him anyway. His burned skin paled and melted from his bones. His eyes popped and rolled like marbles. He lifted a skeleton's arms at me.

"Get ready," the bone-boy said.

I shrieked and snapped my lids tight.

The murky waters rushed in a great wave. I opened my eyes at the sound. Jake was back to being Jake. He pointed at the water ahead of us. Thousands of fatheaded fish bounced on the solid surface. Their mouths chattered gulps in the open air. We continued moving despite our ceased work.

The little canoe rode up onto an invisible ice shelf occupied by endless suffocating fish. The boat tipped and we spilled onto the frozen surface.

A blizzard ensued and I hugged myself against the frigid temperature as I slipped and skidded on the slick pond. Jake prayed to our mother. This time I nearly joined in.

The wind blew the shelf clean beneath us. I pushed forward with my face down against the wind and then I saw them.

"No more," I whined.

Rushing below the ice, high-speed doggie-paddle, the wolves swam and charged their noses against the clear ceiling beneath our feet. The precarious layer cracked and I slipped. It cracked more as I pushed from my knees. Jake tugged on my arm.

"Come on, Austen!"

The cracking ice creaked a horrid din and we splashed down. Close enough to shore that the water only came up to my chest. Jake's neck. The wolves moved faster and gained ground on us. The weather shifted as we approached the shore. Warmer. A summer night once again. Impossibly.

A wolf jumped onto my back. I thrashed and wailed. Its boiling breath singed my throat through the tomato red burn. Jake swung a fist into the wolf's nose and it lost balance. He dragged me ashore like a superhero lifeguard.

"Where can we go?" I screamed at him.

He stared at me with stern and hard eyes. I felt my insides settle. If my little brother could manage then I could too, *sure as shit.*

"Got to move." He tugged me again.

My soggy jeans made it difficult to run. I had trouble keeping up.

"Stop right there, thankless little shits," that familiar voice said. "Ungrateful, lazy, shits, this is the thanks I get, a rock to the head?"

Nathan Abbott's hands landed on both of our necks and we fell to the ground together as if facing matching nooses.

"No! Please, we're sorry!" I sobbed.

"Please, Mommy! Mommy, please!" Jake prayed into his palms.

Nathan Abbott laughed himself into a transformation. It was him all along. The devil from the cabin, playing a monster's game, jumping skins. The snakes and worms danced about his flesh, poked out around his eyes and out of his nose. The wolves circled us, pacing.

Something clicked in me.

The world wasn't logical. It wasn't built on rules. The real world is not solid and calculable, it is murky and improbable. I was too young to have any hard notions about the universe anyway. I was angry. I was ignorant. I was scared.

I put my hands together.

"Mommy, please, dead isn't dead! Dead can't be dead! Mommy!"

The hand left my neck and sky lightened into a great blast of light. The universe changed its course with a great whoosh that roiled into my veins. I felt happiness and love. I felt it all. I understood what my mother had to offer, dead wasn't dead, not always.

I fell forward and cried tears of grace.

Footfalls approached me.

"You all right, boy?"

I opened my eyes and looked up at an unfamiliar man. Then I saw the gas station, the town just one short hill away. Trouble was behind me, and me and Jake beat it. I knew it without doubt. Beat the devil, beat the wolves, beat the elements.

"We had to do it," I said calmly. "He was gonna kill us, we had to do it."

There was no need for tears anymore.

"We who?" the old man asked.

I stood and looked around for the other half of my *we*.

Where the hell? "Jake… Jake!" I screamed.

"Jake? Wait, are you called Austen? You lived with those scumbag Abbotts?"

"Yeah, but we had to do it." It was very important that this old man standing in the gas station parking lot believe my story.

"It's all right, boy."

"Where's Jake? Jake?" I couldn't understand where he'd go. Why he left me.

The old man took me inside the gas station and we waited for the police. I knew for sure I was done. My prayers didn't work without my little brother there.

We drove to the hospital and the officer took me to a weird little room at the back.

"This Jake?" he asked.

I looked down at the dirty face connected to the body on the table. Both his nose and mouth, smashed into barely recognizable shapes. The sun bubbled and scaled a burnt film over his cheeks and forehead. There were several holes in the flesh.

"Doc' says the birds got at him."

It looked just like Jake, but it couldn't have been Jake.

"Appears Nathan Abbott pounded on this poor kid a while. Now that I see you, looks like he pounded on you a while too. I guess then you took a rock and smashed him when he wasn't lookin', that about right?"

"No," I said, coming to my senses. "He was on me, then Jake came with a rock and we went through the forest and over the pond. There was a man in a shack and…" I read the look and I shut up. It was the look adults give to children when they're sure they know better.

"It's okay, son. We aren't going to press charges or anything. Abbott shot his wife right before he went at you. I'd say you're lucky you got'm with that rock."

I wanted to remind him that it was Jake, but it all fell apart in the logistics.

It couldn't have been Jake, not the way the cop knew the world.

Jake had died in that field. I know that now. I don't even question it, but dead doesn't mean dead, not always, for the good ones and the bad ones alike.

END

Dead is Dead, But Not Always

About this book

Bear with me, I have words about my words.

If a story were a child, then, as it is in society, some children get in and fit in with ease, while other children can't quite get along anywhere. Nasty as that is.

In selling fiction, there are dozens of publications at any given time willing to look at your story, your child, your baby, no matter the genre, so long as it falls into the publication's field and then word count... and that you're not advocating for harmful action against your fellow human, et cetera.

The stories in this collection, some of them first penned six or seven years ago now, have been cut and chunked and molded. They were ugly babies too long for most publications to consider and too whatever else to fit in where longish stories go. I'd battled with these ugly babies, trying to make them into things they were not until finally the living, breathing essence within each tale pissed on all my attempts at corralling the word counts and made me right the wrongs I'd attempted with my ham handed cuts.

Soaked and stinking of urine, I felt better. So what if no eyes were apt to fall on them, stuck in my hard drive folders as they were? I have hundreds of stories like that... oh but they do nag, not all of them, but the ones I like. They nag. Those ones nag like crazy.

And guess what, these here pissy babies weren't only ugly nagging babies who kept it at least moderately civil, no way Pedro, these were screaming monsters. Attention they did need and I tried to tell them: only I love you, it's okay, we'll be okay, just you me and the other ugly babies, so shhhhh.

But they weren't to be silenced.

Thank fuck for Facebook.

Imagine someone saying that!

One night, I'm sure it was night because that's when I typically visit the site, Becky Narron and I got to chatting. She suggested I send something to the HellBound Books inbox. I knew they did standalone titles, but open submissions are a tricky bitch. Most places you have to check for when the moon lines up with Jupiter and the your Aunt Hilda gets her period and it's taco day at the elementary school down the block, and only then are submission windows open.

I clicked through to a secondary page on the HellBound site and the word COLLECTIONS started an ugly baby chain reaction. They shouted at me, some had been in folders so long they had dust beards and baritone voices... Eddie, if you don't send us in, we'll climb out of your hard drive, tie you up, and self-publish every piece of garbage you've ever written, we'll even max out your credit cards on advertising so people actually read the shit too. That stupid story about the monster climbing out of the sink drain, and the one with the restaurants where the burgers turn everyone into dragons, and the one about knitting circle that grave robs for free fabric, they'll headline collections of first drafts and aborted missions, and the world will know you're a shit writer!

You wouldn't! I screamed, but I didn't dare tempt these ugly babies. As much as I like them, I don't trust them. So I took a spit rag and shined them up, sent them off, and hoped for the best.

When the acceptance email landed in my inbox, these ugly babies grew silent, because when you find a new home for a baby, it's not a baby anymore. It's out in the world, living its life.

Too often the novelette and the awkward-length short

story get chopped and severed for the sake of an attempted sale. If it does sell, then it was probably the right thing to do, but if it doesn't, it can scream for repair, and once fixed, it screams for a chance at an audience.

The novelette is a length I enjoy reading and writing, but is one troublesome bitch to get out there, so thanks to HellBound for taking on this project.

I would say all's quiet nowadays, but I'd be lying. Fucking novelettes just keep coming.

Eddie Generous

Dead is Dead, But Not Always

Other HellBound Books Titles
Available at:
www.hellboundbookspublishing.com

Psychological Breakdown

Within this tome lies eighteen tales of mind-bending terror, as Hughes delves into the human psyche and dishes out stories of what becomes of the broken minded, spirited and downright irked.

Part these blood-drenched pages at your own peril, for you will find diseased minds geared towards revenge and bloody chaos, with a few twists, turns and surprises thrown in for good, fucked-up measures.

Keep the lights on!

Blood and Kisses

The definitive short story collecting from James H Longmore - an eclectic mix of dark horror, bizarro and Twilight-Zone style tales of the downright disturbing.

Welcome to the long awaited collection from the writer of horror novels *'Pede* and *Tenebrion*; a foreword by Richard Chizmar (co-author of *Gwendy's Button Box* and author of *A Long December*)

18 short stories, 5 flash fiction and even a poem - all skin-crawling, soul-shredding tales of terror, of the darkest things that skulk amongst the night's inky shadows, and of the everyday gone horribly awry.

Discover the alternative implication of technology becoming self-aware, enjoy the acquaintance of a charismatic new pastor who promises his flock a brand new place in which to worship his God, and spend a little time in the company of a nice young man who is inexorably caught up in his home town's terrible secret. Then there is Cupid's revelation that personally he has never experienced love, yet we discover that very emotion alive and not so well amongst the ruins of a post zombie apocalypse world, and we bear witness to a childhood innocence forever destroyed in a war-torn city. There is more, Dear Reader, much, much more; for within these pages we have devils, demons and ghosts, lycanthropes and demi-gods, all rubbing nefarious shoulders with vilest of Hell's offspring who have slithered from the netherworld to doff their caps and wish us all the sweetest of dreams...

Shopping List 2: Another Horror Anthology

Once again, HellBound Books Publishing brings you an outstanding collection of horror, dark, slippery things, and supernatural terror - all from the very best up and coming minds in the genre.

We have given each and every one of our authors the opportunity to have their shopping lists read by you, the most wonderful reading public, and have the darkest corners of their creative psyche laid bare for all to see...

In all, 21 stories to chill the soul, tingle the spine and keep you awake in the cold, murky hours of the night from: Erin Lee, The Truth Artist, John Barackman, Serena Daniels, M.R. Wallace, Isobel Blackthorn, Pamela Morris, Alex Laybourne, Jason J. Nugent, Josh Darling, Jovan Jones, Nick Swain, Douglas Ford, Craig Bullock, Craig Bullock, Jeff C. Stevenson, PC3, David F Gray, Sergio Palumbo, Donna Maria McCarthy, David Clark & Megan E. Morales.

Demons, Devils and Denizens of Hell Vol, 2

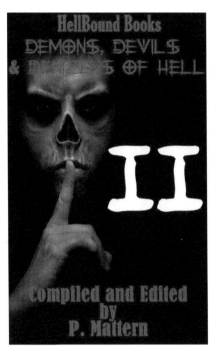

The second volume in HellBound Books' outstanding horror anthology fair teems with tales of Hades' finest citizens – both resident and vacationing in our earthly realm… -

Compiled by the inimitable P. Mattern and featuring: Savannah Morgan, Andrew MacKay, Jaap Boekestein, James H Longmore, Stephanie Kelley, Ryan Woods, James Nichols, P. Mattern, Marcus Mattern, Gerri R Gray, and legion more…

The Big Book of Bootleg Horror 2

The second volume in HellBound Books' flagship horror anthology - this one bursting at the seams with even more fantastically dark horror from the cream of the rising stars in today's horror scene!

Featuring: Tracey A. Cross, Elizabeth Zemlicka, Shelby Thomas, Matthew Gillies, Spinster Eskie, Stephen Clements, Ken Goldman, Nathan Robinson, K.M. Campbell, Cody Grady, Sebastian Bendix, Leo X. Robertson, David Owain Hughes, Timothy McGivney, Kane Gordon, Todd Sullivan, Mike Mayak, Edward Ahern, Rose Garnett, Jaap Boekestein, Brandy Delight, Stanley B. Webb, D. Norfolk, and Thomas Gunther.

**A HellBound Books LLC
Publication**

www.hellboundbookspublishing.com

Printed in the United States of America

Printed in Great Britain
by Amazon